Meet Me on Christmas Eve

Alana Highbury

Copyright © 2023 Alana Highbury

All rights reserved.

The characters and events portrayed in this book are fictitious. Any similarity to real persons, living or dead, is coincidental and not intended by the author.

No part of this book may be reproduced, or stored in a retrieval system, or transmitted in any form or by any means, electronic, mechanical, photocopying, recording, or otherwise, without express written permission of the publisher.

Cover design by Beetiful Book Covers

ISBN-13: 9798867077273

Printed in the United States of America

Content Note

This book contains the following content.

If you'd rather avoid any spoilers, skip this page!

Explicit scenes: None.
Language: Mild to moderate swearing.
Themes: Mental health issues. Previous childhood trauma including poverty and death of a parent. Occasional alcohol consumption.

Dear Marcus, you rock my world.

Chapter 1

With a slow exhale, I smoothed a hand over my straightened hair and met her dark brown eyes. "I told you already, Hazel. This purchase will be a great asset to—"

"Yeah, a profitable addition to Northam Resort and its offerings, blah, blah."

I forced myself to maintain eye contact. "Well, that's it, Hazel. It's a good business decision, plain and simple." While she continued staring at me, I resisted the urge to fidget. "Jeff thinks so too."

My best friend shook her head and gave me a pointed look. "Cut the crap. Jeff is just scared of you."

"He's *what*?" I raised my eyebrows, breaking the pretense of calm for a moment. The idea was ridiculous, that anyone, much less my stuffy financial advisor, could be scared of me. *Me*. "It's—you know it's a good business decision. Maybe a brilliant one."

"It's a *weird* business decision. Sure, it'll make money during the holiday season, but what about the rest of the year? There has to be more to this."

"Well, sure, it's only a Christmas village now, but it doesn't have to sit dormant the rest of the year. It's not—"

"Mariana, please." She went behind me and poked at my upper back and shoulder area a few times. "You're so tense. You were like this when we visited the place last week, and yet … there was something else too." She paused, her voice uncertain.

I let out a long exhale and closed my eyes for a moment. "I … I like Christmas."

She circled my chair to face me. "*You*? Come on, you'll have to do better than that. You've always shown exactly zero enthusiasm for the holiday season."

I almost laughed. "No, I do. I actually kind of secretly love Christmas. So … yeah." I examined my nails, filed to perfection as always.

Her jaw dropped open for a long moment. "I wouldn't believe you. I *couldn't,* except for that telltale blush."

Ugh, the stupid blush. I had spent years refining everything about myself. Getting rid of all the markers of the old, flighty, lower-class Mariana. Learning how to be sophisticated, calm, and unemotional. But my body wouldn't fully cooperate with the mandate, and I occasionally blushed at the worst times.

Hazel narrowed her eyes, putting her hands on her hips. "What do you love about it?"

"I love …" What do I say? It's not any one thing. It's all the little things that make up the holiday season, memories of times long ago, of love and hopes and dreams. And … things I couldn't tell her. "*Jingle Bells*, of course. Who doesn't love Christmas jingles?" I smiled. "Fa-la-la-la-la."

She just laughed, shaking her head. "You think you're such a good liar, Mari, but you're a terrible one. *Terrible*. I will figure this out. You know I will."

I sighed. She probably would. But perhaps I could keep some of my dignity until then. "You're fired," I grumbled. "I'm hiring a new lawyer."

She giggled. "Good luck finding anyone else who'll do it for free while putting up with you."

"Oh, I think I'd pay quite a lot to get rid of my free counsel-slash-thorn-in-my-side," I said irritably. I only half meant it, of course. I was mostly irritated with myself because I was always like this with her. Not the best version of myself, not the refined version I wanted to be. Too messy.

"Don't make promises you can't keep," she said sweetly as she pulled up a chair next to me. "But thanks for confirming … now I know this Christmas stuff must be one hell of a story."

I squeezed my eyes shut. One hell of a story I wouldn't be telling her anytime soon, or maybe ever, best friend or not. At least not the worst of it … that part was staying far, far in the past where it belonged. Where *he* belonged.

"But speaking of holidays, we have that party tonight, remember?"

My eyes flew open. "Wait, no, I—"

"No, you're not backing out. I'm supposed to meet this guy from a dating app there, and I need you in case he's a weirdo. Besides, this is a strategic move for you, Mari. If you really want to expand, you have to establish a presence in the area, outside the walls of this damn place." She paused. "You know it's true."

I scowled because I knew she was right.

*****

"Halloween, of all things. I hate Halloween," I hissed, leaning in so the revelers around us wouldn't hear. I might as well be polite, right—or at least try to avoid actively being a buzzkill to the entire party.

Hazel eyed me in amusement. "But do you really? I used to think you hated all holidays, but turns out that's not true."

I glared at her, while nearly bumping into some idiot dressed like … what was it, even? A pinecone, maybe? "Sorry," I mumbled before quickly turning back to Hazel.

"Next time we'll get better costumes though. I didn't plan this one very well."

We'd just grabbed some very old-fashioned maid costumes from the resort storage closet. Well, she had. I would never have chosen to wear something like this. I would've chosen something with a mask so I wouldn't be recognized. Reputation was important in my business, after all. Running a resort for elite clients meant maintaining a certain upper-class image myself. I had to represent the brand. That was a tall order, considering where I'd come from, but I'd reinvented myself. I was Mariana Northam of Northam Resorts. Mariana LaBelle might as well be dead.

But this version of me wasn't sure how to navigate this social setting. The town of Shipsvold was set in a valley surrounding a lake that provided a great deal of entertainment year round for both the townsfolk and my resort guests. The resort sat just on the edge of the town, on the other side of the lake. Within the small town was a Christmas village, the one I wanted to purchase. In the center was a Christmas-themed shop, and I knew the owner still worked in the shop herself sometimes. Holiday tourism had been dipping in recent years, but I was certain I could revive it while also boosting the amenities for my resort guests if I could somehow offer activities from the village as part of a holiday-themed package. It was a decent business idea, and I could see endless possibilities as I scanned the room at the bar Hazel had dragged me to. I wondered if the village owner would be here. I thought not, as she was much older, but Hazel had said it was a possibility.

"Are you even listening at all?" Hazel asked me.

I opened my mouth to answer but then shook my head. She knew me better than that … which was often both a blessing and a curse.

"We need to mingle," she said, pulling me along as I nearly tripped over my heels. As if maids wear stilettos. At least the skirts hadn't been short. The previous resort owners had been fairly conservative, including with their staff attire.

"Where's this guy you're supposed to meet here?" I asked as she dragged me across the room.

"Oh, I only said that to get you to come with me. Sorry, Mari. But desperate measures, you know?" She smiled.

Desperate? What was that supposed to mean? I wasn't desperate for anything. I was about to ask her, but she'd already moved on. Extrovert that she was, Hazel was starting up a conversation with some random people who looked about our age.

"You can smile, you know," one of the men in the group said to me while flashing a wide smile.

I groaned. I suppose I'd have to be polite, even though the old civilized Mariana was dying to do something very uncivilized, like stick out my tongue. And *then* smile.

Hazel nudged me with a knowing smile. "She claims to not be a Halloween fan."

"Impossible," said a tall, blonde guy next to Hazel looking us both over from head to toe. "What's not to like?"

"Oh, I totally agree, Chad. It's everything you could want in a holiday," said a woman next to the blonde guy, obviously trying to get attention.

Hazel laughed. "Well, everyone but Mari. I had to drag her here." She looked over at me and, seeing my frown, wrapped an arm around my shoulders. "But hey, it's all good because you're here."

I was going to kill her. I would. How was this supposed to help me establish a presence in the area? Now I'd be known as the Halloween Hater. I tried to smile as I shook off her arm.

"Is that true?" said a quiet voice, coming from the pinecone costume that just joined the group standing around us.

"The best part about Halloween," I said with a wry smile, "is when it's over. Because then you get to decorate for Christmas."

Oh crap, did I really say that? I'd never live this down … How strong was this drink Hazel got me? I felt my cheeks heating up, but whether it was a blush or the booze, I couldn't tell. Probably both. Just a cherry-red disaster.

"What? No way, that's way too early," said a woman in the group.

I rolled my eyes. "Let me guess. Thanksgiving at the earliest?" Several people nodded, and I shook my head.

"Wow, you *are* Mrs. Christmas, Mari," said Hazel, looking at me with some awe. "Where have you been hiding all these years?"

Fortunately we had enough extra makeup on that she probably didn't notice my definite blushing at that point.

But the pinecone stepped toward me. "Mari?" As it came closer, I could hear it was a man's voice, a deep rumble, and dark brown eyes came into view through the small eye holes in the costume. Eyes that I—

Oh.

No.

No, no, no. I couldn't breathe. Or speak. Or move. Or … stand. I started to sway toward Hazel, who caught me.

"Mari, are you all right?"

I tried to speak, looking between her and the pinecone costume. A couple of choked sounds came out. I could feel the sweat beading on my forehead, about to drip down my face.

She narrowed her eyes and looked at the man in costume, taking a step toward him. "Look, Mr. Pinecone, I don't know what you've done to upset my friend, but leave Mariana the hell alone."

He merely stood in place, blinking as he looked at her briefly but only for an instant and then resumed staring. At me.

I turned and ran.

Chapter 2

Stupid, stupid shoes. I made it all the way outside before I tripped, landing on my butt in a puddle. It had rained earlier … because of course it had, a cold October rain. And of course I fell.

Only seconds later, he caught up with me. "Mariana?"

I closed my eyes, wanting to disappear into the freezing puddle. So much for my reputation, my dignity, my—

Wait, what the hell was he *doing* here?

I stood up with as much dignity as I could muster, hoping no one walked behind me and saw my wet skirt and tights from behind.

"Yes, I'm Mariana. Northam. And you are?" I was proud of how polite and distant I sounded. I think.

His eyes flashed for a moment. "Mariana Northam," he said slowly, extending the syllables. "Married, wow," he said so quietly that I almost didn't hear. He cleared his throat then. "This—"

"What the hell, man?" Hazel stepped up next to me then, scowling at him. "I told you to leave my friend alone."

"I just—" Something like frustration sounded in his tone. "I just want a moment to speak to her. Is that all right?"

My best friend looked at him for a moment and then at me. I bit my lip.

Would it be better to talk and get this over with? Or use her as an excuse to get the hell out of here? I had no idea if he was here visiting or if … heaven forbid, if he was here for a longer stay. Or if he lived here. He couldn't!

I needed to know.

Even if it killed me.

I took a deep breath and gathered my courage, using a prim voice. "We need to leave, but I can offer you a minute or two of my time first."

Hazel eyed me for a long moment and then whispered, "I'm just going to sit right over there and call a ride. I'll stay within sight."

I nodded, watching reluctantly as she sauntered away, giving him the gesture to let him know she'd have her eyes on him.

Turning to him slowly, I folded my hands in front of me.

I could do this. I'd faced worse than this in my life. Far worse.

"So, you were about to introduce yourself, Mr. …?"

"Terry Grant," he said, his eyes holding mine as he stuck out his hand.

I reluctantly shook his hand, regretting it instantly as his touch brought back so many memories, just the simple touch of a handshake. It was fire, and I was burned. I jumped back quickly.

"But you already knew that." He removed the top of the pinecone costume, which turned out to be a big headpiece.

Oh no, it was him. But it also wasn't.

It wasn't boy-next-door Terry that I'd fallen in love with a decade ago, the one barely of age.

This Terry was all man, all grown up. Square jaw, hard lines, full lips that were currently curved downward. His short, dark hair was just a bit longer on top, but not as floppy and loose as it once was. I thought I saw a couple silver strands around his temples, but maybe it was a trick of the outdoor light.

And once again, I couldn't breathe. Or speak. I tried to focus on my feet planted squarely on the ground, keeping me steady, keeping me from running or, hell, launching myself at him …

"You know damn well who I am, Mariana. Now tell me, why are you pretending you don't?" he demanded. He was angry. His face was red, maybe from the hot mask, but I knew that look in his eyes. I remembered it, along with every other expression. But now it all looked different because he was … *this*. This man.

"I—I wasn't," I stammered. I had no idea what to say. "Are you … you're … Terry," I said the name slowly, the feel of it on my tongue strange, such a long ago memory. "I can't believe it's you," I whispered, still in shock.

For a moment, his face softened slightly, but then it hardened once again as he pressed his lips together. "Well, indeed. I have a similar feeling. Especially since I didn't even know if you were alive."

I winced. I had no excuse to give him, nothing I could share anyway. I opened and closed my mouth several times, unsure how to respond. Finally, I said, "I hope you're doing well. You look … healthy."

Healthy? This had to be the most mortifying day of my life. And I've had many such days before.

One corner of his mouth twitched slightly, but he didn't smile. "I'm in good health, yes. Are you? You look … different." Different? What does that mean? Then, a moment later, he added, "No, what I really want to know—"

"Time's up," Hazel said, swooping in and linking arms with me. I have never been happier to see her. Before he could get another word in, she was dragging me away. "Goodbye, pinecone. Wrong holiday, by the way."

*****

If I thought I'd escaped questioning from my ever-inquisitive best friend, I'd be wrong.

No, I figured it was coming. But I had still hoped.

Last night, I'd managed to convince her I needed to be alone and sleep. Which, obviously, I did. Not to mention some sleep meds to make me forget.

But when I tried to plead illness to cancel our lunch date today, she showed up with soup and orange juice at my door.

"You're such a bad liar, Mari," she said after taking one look at me. "So I'm going to eat the soup."

I watched helplessly as Hazel waltzed in, heading to my kitchen island and setting her food down. Sighing, I went to grab a coffee and made a sandwich as she watched me warily.

"Have you found a realtor yet, by the way?"

Her question surprised me. We hadn't talked about it in a while, and I had hoped she'd forgotten about it. "No."

Her eyebrows rose. "Because … you haven't been looking?"

"Because I've been busy."

She nodded like she didn't believe me, taking a spoonful of soup. "You plan to live here forever?"

What if I did, dammit? This place was my livelihood. What was the point of finding somewhere else to live? It was easier to live here. I didn't have a life outside of work, and that probably wasn't going to change.

I couldn't tell her any of this though.

Because … well, she'd try to do the whole best friend thing and assure me my life could be more than work, blah blah.

Just, no.

No thanks.

I was fine with my life.

More than fine. I like it the way it is. It's a dream, really. It doesn't get any better than this.

I stirred my coffee slowly. "Oh, hey, Roxy had a little delay in sending out the evaluations from the last retreat. She said to tell you sorry."

Hazel didn't seem to hear me. "Anyway, so you know why I'm here."

I looked at her with what I hoped was a blank expression.

"Last night. Spill."

What could I tell her? Hazel knew some things from my past, but not everything. Far from everything. I liked my privacy, but more importantly, I didn't want her to feel hurt that I had my secrets.

Dammit, Terry.

Why now?

"OK, let's start with an easy one: Who's the pinecone?"

If that was the easy question, I was in trouble.

I forced my quivering mouth to form the words, instead of grimacing. "Terry."

"Terry?" Her eyes were alight with interest.

"Yeah."

After a long pause, her eyebrows scrunched together. "And?"

I sighed deeply. "I knew him."

I took two more bites of my sandwich as she stared at me silently.

"Mariana, you can be the most frustrating person on the planet sometimes. You have to give me more than that! *How* did you know him? When? Who the hell is he?"

A shot of pain burst through me, and it must have shown on my face then because she looked guilty for a moment. I quickly recovered though, smiling to signal that I was fine.

"It was so long ago, we were barely adults. I'm surprised he remembers me."

After a moment where she looked away and then back at me, she said softly, "But you remember him very well. Your first love?"

My eyes shifted downward as I took a shaky breath. I needed to get it together. I wasn't a flighty 20-year-old anymore. When I was fairly confident I could speak without my voice breaking, I looked her squarely in the eye, as I'd learned to do —as I'd mastered over the years to project confidence—and lied. "No, nothing like that." I even added a smile as I smoothed my hair, ready to tell a partial truth. "He was just a guest here when I worked here, long ago."

"You're a goddamn liar, Mari," Hazel said, letting out an exasperated breath. "We've known each other for how many years? I'm insulted that you think your facade works with me."

I opened my mouth to refute her words and then closed it. This was the trouble with close friends, people you cared about. It was harder to maintain the image, to be the person I needed to be at all times. I'd survived and gotten this far in life by becoming the new and improved Mariana, who didn't do emotions and messy human stuff—or if I had to, I did it with grace and a polite smile. But I'd be lying if I said part of that survival hadn't also rested on having Hazel as my best friend. Being there for me when the facade crumbled, when it became too much. I wish I wasn't that weak, but I'd learned long ago there was no use lamenting it; I could only work on improving.

I exhaled slowly as I took in her face and body language, which screamed both anger and hurt. "I'm sorry, Hazel."

She stared at me for a moment and then scooted closer to me. "You can be real with me, Mari."

I nodded, looking at my hands in my lap.

"I know you don't *really* hear me when I say this, so I'll keep telling you a thousand more times if I have to. I want the real you."

I struggled to swallow as I tried to stop my fingers from trembling. I felt a burning sensation in my eyes, and I thought back to all the times she'd said this. If she only knew the real me, she wouldn't be saying this.

To my horror, she put her hand over one of mine, which was by now shaking visibly and probably sweaty. "Please let me in, Mariana."

I breathed in a few times, shallow at first and then more deeply. Finally, I looked up, but not at her. "Can I … just have a moment? I need to use the restroom."

She sighed. "OK, Mari."

I smiled to let her know I was fine.

She didn't believe me, but that's fine. She knew me better than I was comfortable with, and sometimes she let me have my space. Sometimes.

I knew this wasn't going to be one of those times though. Hazel wasn't going to let this go.

I stared at my reflection in the wide mirror above my bathroom sink. My cheeks were definitely flushed. From exertion or emotion, I wasn't sure. Probably both. I cursed my stupid genes, for the millionth time.

Did my eyes look bloodshot? I didn't sleep well last night. That's probably why they were stinging. I suffered from dry eye syndrome. I wasn't the crying type; it *surely* wasn't that.

I smoothed my hand over a tiny piece of lint on my shoulder, frowning as I debated whether to go change my top.

Then I noticed it: My blonde, chin-length hair looked … wavy.

Oh, hell no, I thought as I retrieved my straightening iron out of the closet behind me.

*****

I was just turning the straightening iron off when Hazel knocked on the door. "Mari? Are you alive in there?"

I laughed. "You're in luck. I am."

Maybe if I joke with her, she'll forget we were going to discuss something serious.

"Good," she said, opening the door. "I was just—" She halted, looking at me with a strange expression.

"What?" I tried to avoid looking in the mirror to see if something was still out of place.

"You were in here refreshing your makeup?" Her eyes were narrowed, and she looked down and saw the straightening iron still on the counter. "Oh my god, did you just do your hair?"

People like her could never understand why people like me needed to spend a lot of time and energy on hair and makeup and exercise. She was naturally gorgeous. She looked better *without* makeup, and her long dark hair was perfectly straight and just … perfect.

I couldn't get away with the no-maintenance approach she took to appearance. I'd be a troll. Besides, fitting in with an elite crowd meant meeting certain standards, looking polished and refined at all times.

"Just a bit of touching up," I said, unable to keep the defensive note from my voice. "We can't all be naturally beautiful 24/7."

She rolled her eyes. "No, we can't all. But *you* could. You're gorgeous, Mari, when you let go a little."

I gave her a small smile of appreciation as we left the restroom. She was wrong, of course. But she was my best friend, really my only friend, so she had to say these things. And I had to let her, I supposed.

"Come on, let's get cozy by the fire. I made us some hot chocolate."

"Oh, I'm not thirsty—"

She gave me a side-eye glance. "Uh-huh. I'll drink yours if you insist. But come sit. Tell me about Terry."

I sat down on the sofa by her and stared at the steaming mug on the coffee table in front of us. I should say no because, well, I was trying to cut back on sugar. Wasn't everyone? But it might make this whole thing a little easier …

"Or should we call him Mr. Pinecone?" When I broke into a slight grin, she added, "Made you smile."

She was quiet for a long moment as I picked up the mug and took a sip. I looked into the fire, trying to decide what to say, where to even start.

Hazel knew that my childhood hadn't been easy, spending a lot of time in foster care. Many details she didn't know, and I'd take them to my grave if I could.

"I met him a couple years before you. I was working here as a summer job. A temp thing. I was a broke college student, as you might remember." I tried to laugh, as though it was funny and not something I was extremely sensitive about.

She didn't laugh. "So he was here … as a guest?"

I swallowed with some effort. "Yes, he … Terry stayed here with his family for a few weeks that summer. His parents and sister. As you can imagine, like all the guests who come here, his family was, uh, well off. Rich enough to own a house in the Hamptons. But his dad grew up here, so that's why they visited that summer."

"So, you thought he was out of your league?"

"He *was* out of my league. So, so far out. I would never have dreamed … but somehow he ended up interested in me, for some reason. Maybe he was in a stage of rebelling from his family and I was his way of doing that, I don't know."

Hazel's brows furrowed. "Or maybe he just liked you."

"Maybe." But I had never been able to figure out why.

Frowning, she asked, "So, what happened?"

"Well, we had a thing, and then it ended when he left."

Her eyes widened. "I hope you plan on giving me a lot more details than that."

My eyes shifted from her to the fire. "Oh, I don't know if there's much more to tell. I guess we were kind of into each other, but it was really short-lived. And then he left."

"He just left," she said flatly, disbelief on her face.

I sighed. I was hoping to not have to say this bluntly because, well, it was embarrassing. But I needed to be clear with her so she'd get the picture that there was really nothing else to tell. At least, nothing concrete. "I literally never heard from him again."

She was silent for a long time. "But why?" She sat up, leaning toward me. "Didn't you … didn't he—"

She stopped when she saw my face. It was flushed again, I was certain. I didn't want to talk about this. I pleaded with her silently to not make me say this aloud.

"You tried to reach him," she said softly. "And the bastard never responded."

Sensing a hint of moisture in the corner of my eye, I blinked quickly.

"Mari, I'm so sorry. You—"

I sat up straighter, looking away for just a moment and then back at her with a forced smile. "No, it's fine, and I'm fine, Hazel. That's the sordid tale. Not that bad, right? Really not even very exciting, you know me."

She took a few more sips and then set her empty mug

down. "Is this your first time talking to him since that summer?"

I wanted to lie. To say no, or maybe I didn't remember. "Yes." I looked away.

She nodded, seeming unsurprised. "Have you looked him up on socials?"

"No." I didn't even let myself think about him, much less do something as stupid as stalking him on Facebook.

She raised an eyebrow. "Seriously? In all these years, you never did? I don't believe it."

I bit my lip. "I mean, I tried at first, after our ... fling, or whatever it was. I tried to text and call him, with no response. Before he left, I was following him on Facebook and Instagram. But then he unfriended me and eventually blocked me or maybe created a new account. I didn't know, because I couldn't find him anymore."

The look she gave me contained so much sympathy, so much *pity*, that I recoiled in horror.

What was I thinking admitting to all that?

"TMI, right? Now you know the whole humiliating situation."

She tilted her head and eyed me for a moment. "*You* have nothing to be embarrassed about, Mari. It sounds like he's a huge jerk. Not to mention a fool." Then, with her eyes flashing, she added, "I'm regretting that I even let him talk to you for a couple minutes."

"It's not your fault," I said with a sigh. "I mean, who knows, maybe he lives here now and I would've encountered him eventually."

Both of us widened our eyes. "Oh my god," I said, panic coursing through my veins. "What if he lives here now? No, no —"

Hazel came closer, settling an arm around my shoulder. "Mari, I'll protect you from that pinecone jerk, I swear it. He's probably just visiting or something. But if he is living here ... well, maybe we can make that temporary."

I raised an eyebrow. "Uh, how?"

"We can sue him."

I laughed. "What? Sue him for what?"

"I'm sure I could come up with something," she said with a smile as she squeezed my shoulder and then relaxed back on the other end of the couch.

"That's not even your area of law, Hazel," I reminded her, feeling the corners of my mouth curving upward despite the situation. She didn't even run an active law practice, except in her capacity as my counsel. Her main business as a health coach and speaker took up most of her time, and she had loathed corporate law earlier in her career.

A devilish smile graced her heart-shaped face. "The things I do for you."

Chapter 3

Exactly one week later, I was eating an overpriced lobster soup in a pricy restaurant across the lake, just outside the Christmas village, when the village owner eyed me shrewdly and asked where I'd grown up.

I had prepared for a number of likely questions from Jane Christiansen, the village owner, but not for this. Why did she want to know? And more importantly, what the hell should I say?

"I grew up in a small town, probably not one you've heard of. So, Mrs. Chris—"

"I told you, call me Jane," the woman said, sounding a bit irritated as she fluffed her short white curls. "What small town?"

I fought to contain my growing panic. "Salem, a few hours north of here," I said quietly, leaning toward her in hopes that at least no one else would hear. I hadn't wanted to lie; after all, she seemed like the kind of person who could find out the truth if she really wanted to investigate.

"Oh, I … yes, dear. Charming place, or at least it was back in the '50s. So you are a Minnesota girl through and through." She beamed.

I smiled in relief. I guess she just wanted me to prove that I was not some outsider, and I passed the test. I dared not look around me to see what the others were thinking though. I hoped no one had heard this exchange; I heard at least one other conversation happening around me.

Hazel was here as my counsel as usual, along with Jeff and

two other business advisors. Janine, my general manager, was present as well. I didn't really need her for this—or for most things—but Hazel was constantly trying to get me to delegate more and do less of the resort management myself. At least get an assistant, she'd begged. It made sense, in theory, but in practice, doing things yourself was more efficient and effective, I found.

"Honestly, I didn't have high hopes for this meeting," Jane said, louder this time to get the attention of everyone at the table. She looked at me briefly. "But I have to say I'm warming to the idea. I like you, Mariana."

I smiled. "Likewise, Mrs.—Jane."

"Let's meet again next week, after I've had a chance to look this over with my partner." Then she hastily added, "Not a formal business partner exactly, but she's my wife and also my accountant. She'll find all the holes in your offer." She cackled then, the long, dangling earrings on her ears shaking.

Genuine hope sprung up within me, though I knew this was only a first step. "Thank you, Jane. I—"

"No more shop talk," she cut me off, raising her wineglass. Her mouth twisted into a sly smile. "Well, at least not my shop. I want to hear all the latest resort gossip."

I raised my eyebrows and opened my mouth to speak but didn't get a chance.

"Oh, don't look so shocked. We all know that your little hideaway for the rich and famous is not free of salacious happenings."

She was certainly right. We did spend some time dealing with scandals, usually fueled by alcohol and spoiled young people, but sometimes the people embroiled in these situations were the ones you'd least expect. It was the least favorite part of my job—and the main reason I'd finally been convinced to hire a general manager. But discretion was prized at my resort—and I valued it myself highly. The last thing I needed was to tell these stories to a gossipy woman who'd surely tell all the other ladies she knew.

Still … I needed to give her something, if I wanted to win her over.

"Well, there was this one really, really smart guy. He had like three PhDs and had made millions from some tech company …" I looked over at Hazel, and she gave me a lopsided smile. "He ended up crying one night and proposing to one of my staff." This was a fib, as Hazel wasn't really a staff member. And he didn't have that many PhDs. At least I didn't think so. But it made for a more entertaining story and reduced the odds that she'd guess who it was.

Hazel snickered. "Well, he thought he was smart anyway."

Jane looked intrigued and looked back and forth between Hazel and me. "OK, this could be interesting. If you won't give me names, I need other details!"

I smiled, pretending to try to remember and nodding when Hazel gave me a brief nod of approval. Jane may not be hard to convince after all, and the village was well within my grasp.

*****

The Christmas village sat in the heart of Shipsvold, near the lake. This property I wanted to buy contained an outdoor rink, an old-fashioned theatre, decorated garden paths, a large playground, and a central area with a huge Christmas tree and lots of space for outdoor holiday musical events. Last but not least, spanning one whole side of the village was the large holiday-themed shop that was actually a significant tourist attraction in the Midwest.

A few days after meeting Jane, I was scouring this very shop for new decorations when I saw the most beautiful tabletop tree I'd ever seen. It would look perfect in the reception area. Or, hell, maybe I'd just take it for my own room. I decided to find someone who works here to get it boxed up but then got distracted by some gold and red ornaments that I just had to have.

Decorating for Christmas used to be one of my favorite

things ever, and I hadn't done it in years. Sure, the resort had some decorations, but I'd made the staff do it, pretending I didn't care for the holiday. I was planning to go all out this year. And what better way to support the shop in Jane's village than to explore and buy some new decor here?

When my shopping basket was overly full, I decided I should probably call it a day. Rounding a corner to head toward the cashier's desk though, I almost collided with … an elf?

I saw the shoes first, and then my heart skipped a beat—or several—when I looked up and saw the face.

It was him.

My mouth let out some kind of "Ah" sound, and I nearly dropped my basket. My lips started to move, unsure which words to form, as his eyes widened at first and then started to look me over slowly.

What am I doing? I have to get out of here.

With that thought, I spun on my heel and nearly collided with another person, this time a child. I apologized profusely and hoped my face wasn't too red as I finally approached the checkout counter. Fortunately, no other customers were in line, so I dropped my items on the counter quickly.

"Hi," I said to the clerk, a young-ish blonde wearing a Mrs. Claus costume.

"Hi, I hope you found everything you were looking for," she said. Her nametag said Cynthia. I made a mental note, since I'd want to get to know the people here, since they might one day be working for me.

I nodded. "This place is amazing. Oh, I am also interested in that beautiful little tree in the corner by the Christmas socks display. I assumed you'd have a box in the back or something?"

She looked at the computer for a moment and then back at me. "I'll have to go back and check. Or wait, let me ask Terry—hang on."

"Oh—kay," I nearly choked on the words. What? She knew Terry? How well known was he around here? They must be friends or something. Or maybe more? She seemed a little young for him, but maybe he was attracted to young women. Well, good. That meant there would be no chance …

Not that there would be anyway.

Not that I'd care anyway.

Ugh, stop thinking about him.

Or just stop thinking, period.

I put my hand on the counter, willing myself to be calm, serene, the Mariana I'd become.

Finally, she came back, with Terry carrying a large box. My tree. Suddenly, I wasn't sure I wanted it anymore. Was it worth this?

I swallowed. Calm, serene, unemotional. I could do this.

"Found it!" Cynthia said with a smile as she resumed ringing up all my items.

I smiled politely at her, ignoring him. I could feel his eyes on me though as he stood just a few feet away. Why was he still standing there?

"Such a nice day, right? I mean, for November," the cashier asked, looking up briefly before taking more items to scan.

"It is unseasonably warm, yes," I agreed. "A perfect day for apple picking." Not that I would know. I didn't have time for such things. But I overheard another customer saying it earlier.

I watched in horror as the girl's eyes filled with tears. What the hell did I say?

"I … I'm sorry if I said something wrong. Truly, I didn't mean to offend."

She sniffled, grabbing a tissue from under the counter. "No, it's … not …" She paused to wipe her eyes. "It's just, Ben and I were going to go. He—he—" Then a fresh round of tears started.

I snuck a look at Terry, who was looking at Cynthia in sympathy and moving closer to us.

I didn't speak. I couldn't, even if I wanted to. I was incredibly uncomfortable with emotional displays, and I had no idea what to do usually. This one was particularly odd, since she was a complete stranger. Who the heck was Ben?

"You know Ben, right?" she said to me between sniffles.

"Everyone knows Ben." She looked at Terry, who nodded.

Not everyone, I nearly snapped. I didn't know either of them.

Ugh, I didn't know this town very well. And I wasn't doing a very good job of getting to know them. I needed to make a better impression.

"I actually don't, but you can tell me about him if you'd like," I said in a kind voice, or so I hoped.

She looked shocked for a moment but then shook her head quickly. "No, you're lucky if you don't. Screw him. He dumped me last night during dinner with my parents. Who does that?"

"Oh, Cyn, that's the worst," Terry said. "I'm sorry. I gotta say, I've never liked him much."

My eyes widened as I took him in. *Terry knew Ben and Cynthia?* Just how long had Terry lived here? This was alarming. Had he been living here, practically under my nose, for … for as long as I'd been back at the resort, maybe longer than I'd been here? Did he *know* I was back? I felt my pulse racing and my breaths coming faster, so I dug in my purse for my credit card and shoved it into Cynthia's hand, hoping to hurry things along.

"Sorry, that was super unprofessional … Mariana," she said, after looking at the name on my card and then handing it back to me. "I swear I don't usually cry to customers. Well, maybe I sometimes do. I'm sorry though. I hope you enjoy your new purchases!"

"I will, and it's all fine." It's not fine, I thought, and this girl probably shouldn't be working in retail. She might need to look for another job when I bought the place. I'm sure she was sweet, but I couldn't have someone this volatile on the front lines of my business. We might be able to find other work for her at the resort—as a laundress or something less visible.

I looked at the giant box Terry was still holding. "I'll come back for that. Let me just bring these other bags to my car, and I'll—"

"Oh, Terry can probably carry it out for you," she said.

Oh hell no. "No thanks, I'll just—"

"I'm on my way out anyway," he said, his voice sounding deeper than it used to, but it had been a long time so maybe I just didn't remember well. "It would be my pleasure."

My eyes flicked up to his at that comment, and I thought I saw a devious flare for a second, but it was gone in a flash, replaced by a blank look.

I knew I'd look like a jerk or at least an idiot if I turned down his help, so I sighed, thanked Cynthia, and grabbed my bags before turning to speed-walk toward the door.

My car was parked about 50 yards from the shop, and I nearly ran to it, grateful the fall weather hadn't produced any slippery ice or snow yet.

After I opened the trunk and put my bags inside, Terry handed me the box, which I put inside, careful to leave space around the bags so nothing would be damaged.

I thought he'd walked away, but I couldn't be so lucky.

No, he was standing in front of the driver's side door. Leaning against it, actually.

I walked up to him, stopping a few feet away. "Thanks for bringing out the box. I need to be on my way now."

He looked at me and crossed his arms over his chest. "You're welcome."

"So, uh, I need to go."

"Yeah, you said that already." He just stared at me.

What the hell? "So, I need you to please move, so I can get into my car," I explained in a patient voice, like I was talking to a child.

This got him standing up a little straighter, but not moving out of the way. He sighed and ran a hand over his jaw. "Mariana, I was … it was nice to see you. At the party. Then today … both so unexpected. I kinda got the impression you weren't all that thrilled to see me though, were you?" he asked, scratching his head. That beautiful head, which had only gotten a million times more handsome over the years.

Was he really asking me that? Before I could think, I blurted, "Well, you ghosted me, so—"

He laughed, an edge in his voice. "Oh, did I? That's not how I remember it."

I glared at him, and as I spoke, I started to feel out of breath. "Don't pretend you didn't. But it doesn't matter." Then, for good measure, I shrugged and looked at my watch. "I had totally forgotten about you until that Halloween thing anyway."

When I looked back at him, his eyes were focused on me still. I couldn't read him though. "Well, I—I should go," I said, starting to move a bit closer, waving my hands in a gesture indicating he should move.

He didn't move though, and I stopped in my tracks, not wanting to get too close to him. I couldn't make that mistake. Ever.

"What are you doing?" I asked, the voice sounding like someone else.

His mouth twitched for a brief moment. "Talking to you."

My lips parted and then closed. I wanted to ask *Why* but … oh, screw it. "Why?"

"Why not?"

My brows scrunched together, I shook my head. "Fine. Lovely weather we're having. Are you looking forward to Thanksgiving, Terry?" I asked in an obviously fake polite voice.

"Immensely, Mariana," he said with a smirk. He stared at me with those piercing dark brown eyes, and his expression became serious. "And how's your life? What are you doing nowadays?"

Wow, he went there.

I don't want to tell him.

I don't have to tell him anything.

Well, I guess if he lives here, he's going to find out soon enough, if he doesn't already know and isn't pretending.

I sighed and pointed toward the lake. "Northam Resorts. It's mine."

His jaw dropped so fast I thought it must have hurt. OK, so he definitely hadn't known. "You—*you* run the resort? The … the one where we met?"

I'd have to ignore that last part. "Yes, I run Northam. I've owned and run it for several years now." I leveled him with a forced smile. "You look astonished. Is it that shocking that I would become successful in life, Terry?"

He scoffed. "No. I mean … I had no idea." He made a face then, as if trying to puzzle out in his mind how he hadn't known about this. I wondered how long he'd been living in the area.

"And how about you, Mr. Grant? How's the family and the trust fund?" I couldn't keep the sarcasm out of my voice, and I wasn't sure I wanted to.

His face fell, as though I'd stabbed him. I felt something sharp in my own chest. "All gone, except for Blair."

"Oh, where did they go?" I tried for sincere politeness this time.

His jaw clenched, he looked at me and said more loudly this time, "I said they're *gone*."

I couldn't breathe. Did he mean … had they died? "Do-do you mean—"

His jaw ticked again, and he sighed. He looked away for a long moment and then back to me. "My parents died the same year I met you, a few months later. Terrible accident. It's just Blair and me now."

Blair was his sister, who had never liked me, though she pretended she did in front of Terry. "I'm so sorry," I said quietly.

"It's OK. It was so long ago," he said, looking off into the distance. "I don't really want to talk about it."

"OK." The other part of what he'd implied sunk in then. "Do you mean the trust fund is gone too then?"

His eyes met mine again warily. "The family fortune was decimated, yes. But don't go feeling sorry for us. Grants always land on their feet."

"Oh," I said, unsure how else to respond to that. "So, you're really into costumes, eh?" Humor wasn't really my thing, but I felt like I needed to lighten the mood somehow. I could hate him, but I'd still feel bad for anyone who lost their parents. I certainly knew what that felt like.

At this, the corners of his mouth turned up a bit. "Well, tis the season."

Realization dawned then. "Wait, do you *work* in the shop?" Had his fortunes really sunk that low? Not that working in a shop was *low* exactly, but his family had been flat-out *rich* before. Like filthy rich.

"No, I just walk around wearing an elf costume for fun, Mariana," he said, a playful look on his face. "Of course I work there."

My eyes widened slightly, and then I nodded. This would be another staffing change I'd need to make because there's no way in hell I'd have *him* working for me. But this reversal of our fortunes was … jarring. Interesting. Awkward. He had to feel it too.

"Eh, it is what it is."

Oh crap, had I said any of that out loud? "What?"

"You said it's awkward." He looked slightly amused as he studied me. "I'm guessing from your face that you didn't realize you'd said it out loud. Well, I guess some things haven't changed. You used to do that all the time."

Another trait of the old, unrefined Mariana I thought I'd left behind but hadn't, apparently. He must bring out the worst in me.

After a tense silence where I realized I was probably frowning, he crossed his arms and asked, "Am I beneath your notice now, Mari?"

Hearing him call me by my nickname was so jarring that I gasped. Or maybe it was the insinuation that I was … what, a snob?

I looked him in the eye, raising my chin. "What is that supposed to mean?"

"Your nose is literally in the air. Can you see me all the way down here?"

"You're taller than me, you oaf."

"See?"

I rolled my eyes. "You're wasting my time."

His eyebrows rose. "*See?*"

"That's not—" I stopped. This was pointless. I took a step forward. Maybe I'd just try to push him. I was getting desperate. I *had* to leave. "Please move."

He just looked at me, his eyes penetrating my soul. "Are you thinking maybe you can force me to move?"

How was he reading my mind? Infuriating man! "Maybe."

"Go ahead and try. I'd enjoy that." His eyes held a sense of daring.

I took a step back. No way in hell. "No, thank you."

We stared at each other for a long time, and I hated how fast my pulse was racing, how red I knew my cheeks must be.

Finally, he moved out of the way. "I liked the old Mariana better."

"Of course you did," I said, my tone seething. "She adored you and hung onto your every word like a lovesick puppy." I wanted to add *whom you then abandoned*, but I still had some pride.

"Maybe. Or maybe I liked that she wasn't an ice queen." With that parting shot, he strode away.

Chapter 4

An ice queen? Seriously? I'll give him an ice queen. If I ever see that jerk again, I'm going to make it clear how little he meant to me, how beneath my notice he is now—and not because of his financial status but just because of the jerk he is. I'll show him the ice queen. I'll—

"Mari, sorry I'm late," Hazel said, striding into my office.

I jumped a bit, startled from my dark reverie. I'd been ruminating for far too long about the run-in with Terry yesterday. What I should be doing is assessing my emotions and determining how to avoid such a colossal emotional disaster again, but instead, I'm focusing on him. I frowned as I thought of all the time wasted this morning.

"You look like you're in a bad mood. Or is it because I'm late?" she asked. She looked contrite, which was unusual for her. I was immediately suspicious.

"No, it's fine. I'm fine. What's up, Hazel?" I peered at her closely as she sank into the sofa in my office.

"Come, sit," she said, waving me over. Once I was seated next to her, she started, "So, slight bump in the road. Jane is waffling."

What I loved about Hazel was her directness. Though it was sometimes jarring, it never left me wondering or impatient. Still, I was surprised. "Huh. I really felt things were going in a great direction when we met. How serious is this?"

"It's ... well, could be serious. I don't want to speculate. We have some work to do." She kicked off her shoes and put her feet under her.

I inhaled and then exhaled slowly. "OK," I said slowly. "Lay it on me."

"She's not agreeing to the initial proposed terms. She's not sure if she wants to sell at all." She paused. "We have to convince her."

I wet my lips. "OK, let's get Jeff, so he can run numbers—"

"Not with money. She doesn't seem to care about that as much as she cares about the … legacy of the place."

I nodded slowly. "Oh. So, she wants to see our business plan? I wasn't quite prepared to put together something really detailed at this point, but I guess we could come up with—"

"Maybe, but I think you should start thinking about this in a more … holistic way. She loves this place and wants to see it grow or at least be maintained with the unique charm it has, so I don't know if numbers and business plans are what will excite her. It's probably necessary, but I get the sense … with her personality, you might have to win her over personally too. With yourself. Your ideas. You."

I'm sure if I could've seen my own face then, it would've become a picture of horror, as I did not like what I was hearing. At all.

I dealt in numbers and plans.

That was me.

Not people stuff.

Of course, I managed well enough with the people skills when needed, but with a woman like Jane? I was about as likely to succeed with that as I was to win the lottery. Less, probably.

"Oh, Mari, all is not lost."

I raised my eyebrows. "Really? It sounds like our chances are slim."

"No, we just need to wow her."

"Yeah, like I said, chances are slim," I said glumly. "I know myself, Haz, including my own weaknesses. I don't wow people."

She smiled at me. "Oh, but Mari, you do. In a way that is just *you*." I felt a pang of something in my chest area. It felt suspiciously like a sentimental feeling, and I didn't know what to do with that. So I ignored it, as I do with most feelings.

"Thank you," I mumbled, feeling awkward. "But you know what I mean."

"Well, you have me." She grinned. "And a lot of people who are paid to help us look good. We can do this, Mari."

"How?"

"I have no idea," she said with a twinkle in her eye and a flip of her long hair. "Let's have some wine tonight and make a plan."

I had to laugh. There's nothing I love better than a good plan. "That's a terrible idea, but OK."

Chapter 5

After stepping out of our cars, Hazel linked arms with me, and I gave her a grateful smile. "Thanks for arranging this. I know the Tuesday before Thanksgiving isn't ideal, but the sooner we talk to Jane, the better. I need to know what we're up against."

"And you think I'm your best bet for charming her," my friend said with a laugh. "But she liked you at that dinner. We can work with that."

I nodded, looking at the scene around us. It was snowing lightly and really quite beautiful. We were walking to a cafe near the Christmas shop, per Jane's request. She claimed to be happy to meet with us, but she'd stated in no uncertain terms that she wasn't likely to be swayed by a meal.

Well, we could still try.

I had to try.

This place, it just felt … right.

I didn't like to base business decisions—or any kind of decision, really—on feelings. But this one felt like a feeling worth listening to. I couldn't explain why.

I just needed to make this happen.

Hazel somehow knew all this about me. I turned to smile at my best friend, who I really needed to appreciate more. "What time are you arriving in Tokyo?"

She yawned. "With the layover, it's around 7 tomorrow night. I think that's super early in the morning for you—remember the huge time difference."

"Any big plans yet?"

"The usual, Dad and I are going to eat turkey and rice and watch movies with fuzzy socks and booze. Hoping Halley comes, but who knows with her. She said she'd at least do the Christmas thing on Friday. I'm planning to hold her feet to the fire."

I gave her a dubious look. She missed her younger sister, but she never really followed through on any of these threats.

"Hey, I know what you're thinking, Mari, but you're not the only one who loves Christmas. I may have been raised some weird hybrid Jewish Buddhist, but I'm as much of a closet Christmas lover as you are, I think. Or maybe not so closet … you just haven't noticed all these years." She smirked. "I decorated my apartment last year, don't you remember?"

Now that she reminded me, I do recall the decorations, and I'd felt a twinge of … something. Envy, maybe. I had shoved it down. Deep down. Where the other useless feelings went.

"I mean, I grew up here, so I was surrounded by Christmas just like everyone else. I didn't hate it. My parents were trying to fit in with American culture and went all out with the decorating. For *every* holiday, but especially Christmas. When things got worse with them, in the years before the divorce … well, the holidays were the only time Mama didn't seem mad at Dad. It was nice." She paused, looking at me with a half-smile. "But that's in the past. We are going to rock around the clock this year and own Christmas, dammit."

I laughed, her enthusiasm infectious.

"Hello, girls."

We turned to the side to see Jane Christiansen standing with another woman.

Did she hear what we'd said? I groaned inwardly. That was not a very professional start to our meeting.

"Jane, so lovely to see you again!" Hazel said, striding toward her with a bright smile as I rushed to keep up.

"Yes, lovely." She eyed us both, and I couldn't read her expression or her tone.

"Thanks for meeting with us," I said politely, and my eyes

drifted briefly to the older woman at her side and then back to Jane.

The other woman nudged Jane, who then grinned. "Oh, suppose I'd better introduce my other half. Girls, this is Nina."

I stuck out my hand to her. "I'm Mariana Northam, and this is Hazel Tanaka-Katz."

Nina's eyes widened. "Wait, you don't mean … you're not *the* Hazel Katz, are you?"

Hazel grinned. "I am."

Nina looked at Jane and then back at us. "I love your work. I own all your books, and I even went to one of your retreats a year ago. I … wow, it's really you!"

As she continued gushing to my best friend the minor celebrity, I eyed Nina curiously. There was something slightly familiar about her. Did I remember her from a retreat? It seemed unlikely, as I usually wasn't very involved in the running of Hazel's events, but I suppose it was possible. Though she could practice law, Hazel was much happier in her career as a successful and fairly well-known mental health coach and body positivity activist. People called her a cross between Brene Brown and Geneen Roth, and the resort hosted many of her events. Her assistant, who organized all her events both in and out of Minnesota, was even part of my staff—even though Hazel wasn't, technically.

"How much longer are we going to stand outside?" Jane cut in, sounding grumpy. "This fabulous hair of mine doesn't withstand snow very well."

"Apologies, Mrs. Chris—I mean, Jane," I said, taking her gently by the elbow. "Let's head inside, and we'll find a comfortable place to sit down. Maybe by the fireplace?"

Her eyes narrowed at me. "This place doesn't have a fireplace. Haven't you ever been here before?"

Oh, crap.

"I have—yes, I definitely have. It's just been a while. I mean … you know, I think it was just so pleasant and warm last time that I assumed there was a fireplace. The delicious coffee must have distracted me." I pasted a smile on my face.

Her lips twisted into a frown. "Meh, the coffee is just OK. I need to talk to someone about that. Now the tea, you won't find better. The scones, perfect."

Hazel chimed in then. "I love the cinnamon scone."

"I gave them my recipe, you know," Jane said, her mouth forming a slight smile as she eyed Hazel.

"You must be an amazing baker then," I said.

She ignored me though, instead asking Hazel if she liked any of the other scone flavors. I sighed. Well, it's a good thing I'd brought Hazel along.

Nina looked over at me briefly, curiosity in her expression, and then she put her arm around Jane as the hostess walked us over to a table, with Hazel and me following right behind them.

"Not near a window, please. Your warmest seats in the house, please," I said to the hostess, loud enough for Jane to hear me. But did she turn around or acknowledge my efforts?

No, of course not. Not then, and not during the entire meal.

Something wasn't right.

I was going to lose this deal.

At this point, there wasn't even a deal to lose. Not even close.

*****

Outside the cafe, Nina gave Jane a quick kiss and said goodbyes to Hazel and me.

"Thanks for agreeing to visit with us some more today, Jane," I said, offering my hand to her as we stepped down the curb with a thin layer of snow. We were walking to our car, which was parked closer to the Christmas shop, since the cafe didn't have any parking right outside.

"Well, it's either that or go home and endure Nina's soap operas," Jane said, her lips twisting into a reluctant smile. "This seemed like a slightly better option. I hope you're responsible drivers."

"Of course," I assured her. As we approached the shop, I started my pitch. "So, I was hoping to tell you a bit more about my vision for the Christmas village, and the shop really features prominently in that vision. When we go inside, I think I can lay it out for you better."

"Trust me, Jane, she can," Hazel said, squeezing Jane's hand slightly.

Jane nodded warily. "Go on."

I took a deep breath. I couldn't blow this chance. "By all accounts, Christmas is—"

"*Janie!*" came a deep voice from behind.

My heart sank. I knew that voice.

Apparently Jane did too, because she halted and turned. "Well, if it isn't Mr. Grant." She leaned back and whispered to me, "The handsome one … I knew the elder, and he wasn't much to look at, trust me."

She knew Terry's father? Interesting. I might've laughed at her brutal honesty if I hadn't been so dismayed by Terry's appearance. *Again.* He had the worst timing.

Worse yet, he knew Jane. This couldn't be good.

"Janie, the loveliest lady in Shipsvold. Or maybe Minnesota." His face transformed into a smile.

I nearly gasped and had to look away immediately. He couldn't … he shouldn't be allowed to smile. What the hell. Why is he trying to torture me?

Jane was giving him her cheeks to kiss, and she returned the smile, happier than we'd seen her all day. We had managed to thaw her a bit during lunch, though she'd still maintained that she wasn't at all sure she wanted to sell.

"Say, Terry, do you know these girls?" She pointed to us on either side of her. "I just met them, but apparently they've lived up there in the castle for a while."

I fought the urge to roll my eyes. I'd heard the resort jokingly called a castle before, and it was always said in a demeaning way. And anyway, Hazel didn't live there. She had an apartment in town, actually.

I dared to look at Terry, whose eyes were on me, his expression unreadable. "Yes, I know them. A bit."

I had to unclench my teeth and fight the urge to glare at him. He didn't look as though he was happy to 'know' us, and if Jane knew him well, his impression might matter to her. I was going to have to play nice. "We did have the pleasure of meeting Mr. Grant a few times recently." I smiled at both of them.

Hazel nodded. "What a *pleasure* it was." I noticed when Jane wasn't watching, Hazel glared at Terry. And this made me smile genuinely. She had my back, always.

"Oh, silly me, yes, I forgot you mentioned you know Marian," Jane said, patting Terry on the arm that she held onto.

He … what? My eyes widened, darting to meet his. He merely raised a cocky eyebrow before looking back at Jane.

"I was actually just heading home. Would you like a ride home, Janie?" the smug jerk asked her.

No, no, he was *not* going to take away this opportunity. I had to talk to her—I had to—

"You know, gals, I'm tired." She looked at me and then at Hazel. "I don't know if you're good drivers yet. We'll talk sometime. Terry, I'm all yours."

When they'd left, I sighed deeply. "What is it about her and safe driving?" I asked, my tone grumpy. I was feeling petty, not a familiar feeling for the sophisticated Mariana. Who was I lately? Ugh.

"Maybe she or someone she loved was in an accident," Hazel said thoughtfully.

The guilt rushed in. "You're right."

Once we were in the car, I covered my face with my hands.

"Oh, Mari," Hazel said, patting my back. "It'll be all right."

I looked up, sighing. "What are the odds that he didn't influence her sudden change of mind?"

Hazel opened her mouth to speak and then clamped it shut.

"Yeah, that's what I thought." I frowned. "They obviously

know each other well, and not just in a shop owner/employee relation. He called her *Janie* … and she trusts him to drive her?"

"And apparently he talked to her about you," Hazel said thoughtfully. "I wonder what was said. Like, did he share that you were romantically involved or just keep things vague …"

My heart gave a little pang then at the words "romantically involved." I was trying so hard to not think of him that way at all, even in a past sense. I couldn't get distracted by those kinds of thoughts. I couldn't afford to, because distract me they would. It took me far too long for Mariana LaBelle to get over him all those years ago, and Mariana Northam definitely didn't have time for that. I didn't *do* emotional excess.

Then why did I feel like crying?

Surely it's because I felt like the Christmas village was slipping through my fingers. "Is Terry working against me on this? If he has her ear … well, this whole thing could be doomed." I didn't know whether to sob or scream. But I couldn't do either. That wasn't me. I cleared my throat. "Let's call a strategy meeting Friday with Jeff, Janine, everyone. You can call in remotely—"

"Woah, woah. It's a holiday weekend, remember? Give everyone a chance to rest for a few days. Give *yourself* a break, Mari," my best friend said.

My brow furrowed. I didn't want her to be right, but … ugh, I suppose she was. This would have to wait because of the stupid holiday.

OK, I didn't hate Thanksgiving. True, I didn't love it either. And this time, it stood between me and my goals. I'd spend it alone, probably working or reading.

But I didn't hate Thanksgiving.

Chapter 6

I decided I hate Thanksgiving.
Turkey was good, I guess. I usually spent the holiday alone, like most holidays. And that was fine because I was introverted, I'd been doing it a long time, and I liked my own company, usually.

But tonight, not so much.

I wasn't an eggnog person, despite being a fan of Christmas. There's just something about it that's gross to me. But last year, Hazel made me go to a Christmas party that was dreadful—there was nothing Christmas about it, unfortunately—and I'd been so bored that I'd tried spiked eggnog. It was a revelation. So different from plain eggnog.

Tonight, I stupidly poured myself a glass of eggnog and brandy. Not a little shot glass, but a big drinking glass. It tasted so good, so sweet and smooth, that I didn't realize I was … well, let's just say imbibing a little too much, too fast.

Certainly I was plenty old enough to know my limits with alcohol, but the truth was, I didn't drink that much, either in quantity or in frequency. Booze had a tendency to loosen lips and bring forth emotions out of nowhere, making me feel like the old Mariana. No thank you.

So, I was pretty damn angry at myself when I realized how drunk I was only three-quarters of the way through the glass.

I would blame it on the damn rom-com movie that was distracting me. It was no *Pretty Woman*, but it was cute and had me occasionally laughing out loud, which I didn't often do when watching movies or reading fiction.

Well, I didn't watch movies or read fiction very often. Why would I? It didn't further my goals at all. And those activities were all about eliciting emotions. So, not my thing. But occasionally I'd indulge because ... everything in moderation, right? Plus, I had to be reasonably conversant in the latest pop culture, such as movies, so I could relate with my guests, who were often well-read and well-traveled. Some of them were even well-known authors, actors, or other important people. I even had some A-list visitors from time to time. I couldn't afford to be totally ignorant about the things most people cared about.

This movie was a typical will-they-won't-they, and I got hooked immediately.

So, yeah, self-control fail tonight.

To make matters worse, just when the on-screen couple were finally about to kiss, my buzzer sounded.

I groaned. Who the hell was at the door? I'd told the staff I was taking the night off.

I opened the door slowly, being careful to project my usual air of authority so they wouldn't suspect I was well and truly intoxicated. A tall, barely dressed woman stood at the door. She was gorgeous, but she looked pissed. "Can I help you?" I asked.

"Yeah, I was told to come here, you're the boss or something, right?" She chewed her bottom lip. She looked kind of familiar, actually.

"Who told you—never mind, doesn't matter." I'd find out later. She must be someone important. "Yes, I'm the owner, Mariana Northam. What can I do for you?"

"Stacy. Immers. So, my boyfriend, well, my *ex*—" She rolled her eyes.

"Wait. *Stacy Immers*, oh, I knew you looked familiar! Sorry I didn't recognize you at first, but it's been a long day." Yikes, that was a misstep. She was a supermodel, and she was probably the type of person to leave a low review of the resort if we didn't recognize her and fall at her feet every time a staff member encountered her.

"Yeah," she said, waving her hand dismissively. "So, Jesse, my ex. You know Jesse Cane?" She paused, while I nodded, in shock. "We just broke up, and he's acting like a lunatic. I kicked him out, but I guess he needs another room or something. He's wasted. I don't want to get him arrested or anything, but … well, the front desk person said to come find you."

I nodded again, still trying to process that Jesse Cane was here. He was an A-list actor, more like A+ really, and though we'd had those as guests before, it wasn't very often. This could go really well for us, or it could go really badly. Depending on how I handled this. Ugh, how should I handle this? "Yeah, we try to handle things internally when possible, don't worry." I smiled reassuringly at her. "First, what can I do to make *you* comfortable?"

Stacy smiled her expensive smile at me, and I knew it wouldn't be too hard to win *her* over at least. Hopefully Jesse wouldn't prove too difficult either.

*****

An hour later, I'd managed to get Jesse into his own suite, with the help of some staff. We were fully booked for the holiday week, but I kept a few rooms open for emergencies—which this was. I couldn't have someone like Jesse Cane bringing a bad reputation to my resort. Sure, his antics would put our name out there, but I didn't want that kind of publicity. Northam was an exclusive retreat for the elite, and we didn't advertise in the tabloids. For that reason, the PR team under my direction spent a fair amount of money and time on damage control when celebrities were staying here. If I played my cards right though, they would also recommend us to their wealthy, influential friends later, and that's the kind of advertising that helped us thrive.

With this in mind, I'd kept one staff member in the room with me to help Jesse into bed and arrange some other necessities nearby.

I looked at Jesse, who seemed halfway to sleep, and then

at the security staff. "Joi, can you get a couple of water bottles from the fridge?" I was about to go close the shades when a hand gripped my arm.

"Virgin Mary, maybe you can tuck me in?"

I closed my eyes in irritation. He'd been calling me that since we found him, since he said I was too straight-laced and didn't want to get drunk with him. Little did he know I'd already drank plenty that night, though this whole incident had sobered me up a bit. "I can help you with the blanket, sure," I said primly.

After I pulled it over him, he started dragging my hand under the blanket. I pulled it back, obviously, because as tempting as that might be—he was ridiculously handsome and a *movie* star—I was on the job and I didn't just do random hookups.

He made a pouty face and then grabbed my hand again, firmer this time, with a strength that surprised me, given how wasted he was. I was forced to sit on the bed next to him. This time though, he brought my hand to his lips and kissed my fingers. "Sweet Mary, will you stay with me?"

The look in his eyes was haunting, and I hesitated for just half a second.

Fortunately, Joi returned then. "Mr. Cane, we'd better let you get some sleep."

I pulled my hand back gently and then patted him on the head. Wow, he had great hair. Almost as good as—

No, drunk brain, don't even think it. Not him.

"Jesse," I said, wishing I didn't have to use his first name. I'd long ago realized I had better luck using first names with certain clients though, as it helped if they saw me as a friend or peer. "My colleague is right. You need to rest. You'll thank us in the morning." I offered a smile as I rose.

"Doubtful," he retorted. "I'll have the headache to end all headaches."

I pointed to the nightstand. "We've left some water and ibuprofen here on—"

"I need a real drink."

"With all due respect, Jesse, you have had plenty of

drinks." When he looked crestfallen, I said softly, "I get it, you know. The desire to drink to forget someone. But drinking more won't help you forget her—you'll only feel worse." Oh, did I ever get it.

He clenched his jaw and then looked me in the eyes, his blue eyes sad. "It's not her I need to forget. It's *you*. You, the beautiful goddess Mary …" His eyes started fluttering then.

I blinked a few times, shocked. He can't possibly be saying he's more interested in *me*, even for a moment, than in his beautiful ex, Stacy. His judgment must be more impaired than I thought. I attempted a smile. "Shh, just sleep."

I inched away from the bed as he fought sleep, apparently having given up on wooing me, or whatever that was. "Joi, can you take it from here?" I whispered.

I didn't wait for an answer as I slipped out of the room and then out of the suite.

What was that? I asked myself at least a dozen times on my way back to my own rooms. Fortunately, I didn't see anyone else. As soon as I returned to my room, I texted the control room and let them know I'd be unavailable the rest of the evening except in the most dire emergency. I kicked off my shoes and whipped off my business suit, which had me feeling sticky and hot. I threw on a tank top and sleep shorts and poured another glass of eggnog before heading to the couch.

What was that? I had felt strangely sorry for Jesse Cane, the privileged, ridiculously good-looking actor. I rarely feel anything like empathy in these situations. Usually it's apathy or complete detachment, and it served me well to handle them with tact and make good decisions. We'd rarely had any scandals, at least not that the public had known about. But Jesse had touched something within me. Was I attracted to him? Well, sure, of course he was attractive. Insanely so. But I mostly felt sad for him. I knew how futile it was to pine after someone. Someone who …

Well, someone who didn't love you back.

Someone who moved on, who forgot about you easily.

I knew all too well what that was like.

But the parallels between my story and Jesse's were so slim—it was odd that I was connecting the two at all. Was I that desperate?

I sipped some more, feeling the heady rush. I shouldn't have more, but ...

I'm tired of always doing what I *should*.

With a self-satisfied smile, I took a longer drink from the glass. Looking out the window I'd left open, I stared out at the snowflakes. I loved a good snow, as long as I didn't have to drive in it. Or clean it up. Snow was an essential part of the holiday season for me, and as a child, I'd always felt a little cheated if I woke up on Christmas morning and there wasn't any snow on the ground. Of course, this was Minnesota, so there usually *was* snow. And lots of it.

I pictured the Christmas village, all snowy and white. Ice skaters were on the pond, and some kids and their parents were sledding. Colorful lights and wreaths and holly were hung everywhere—as far as the eye could see, if you were standing in the center. And the tree, the grand tree ...

And slowly, as I envisioned the beautiful scene, I saw it all fade in my mind, like I couldn't stop it, like a waking nightmare.

Breathing heavily, I sat up straighter. What was I going to do? I needed the village to be mine. I needed to convince Jane to sell. Did she think I was going to transform it into something hideous or bulldoze it or something? I thought we'd successfully assured her of our good intentions, but maybe she didn't believe us. Could I convince her?

Was it possible? I slumped back again. Was it even worth it? I could convince someone of anything with numbers and plans and money and logic. But Jane didn't care about all that. What could I even offer her? Should I even try?

Why does this even matter so much to me?

But even as the question came to me, I felt a sharp pang in my chest. I knew.

I closed my eyes, seeing his auburn hair and beautiful blue

eyes and thick lashes, so like mine. I saw his smile, and it broke my heart because he offered it so freely, without reserve and without any conditions. And he never smiled more than he did at Christmas. Dad loved the holiday almost as much as he loved me. Even though we had so little, he somehow put a few presents under the tree, every year. He might have wrapped up a shiny rock, but coming from him, such a gift meant everything to me.

When it got to the point where his heart condition couldn't be managed at home and he had to move to a care facility, my heart broke for him. His independence had meant so much to him, and I was all he had. We had no other family, as far as I knew. Though life in foster care wasn't great, I showed up every Christmas with the brightest smile. For my dad.

He was my world.

I realized tears were streaming down my face as I thought of that last Christmas with him, when I was 10. His condition had worsened, and I was so scared. Terrified that it could be the last time I saw him. Hoping, praying to every god that I had heard of, pleading with the universe to spare my father. But through the fear, the absolute terror, I smiled. For my dad.

He was my everything.

Life without him went on much as it did before. I didn't love living in foster care, but I was used to it. We celebrated Christmas, and it was enjoyable, I suppose.

It wasn't the same, of course. Not without Dad.

In my earlier years of foster care, I was moved around a lot. But in my later teens, I stayed with the same family for several years. Lisa Jackson was a pretty good foster mom, by all accounts, and her biological daughter Rhonda even became a friend. They were a well-to-do Black family living in a St. Paul suburb, and for once in my life, I had everything money could buy. But more importantly, I had what felt like a real family—they cared about me. I even started to enjoy Christmas again with them.

A fresh wave of tears emerged as I thought about the three of us sitting in front of the fireplace eating frosted Christmas cookies. Life was good with the Jacksons. But when I was 17, Lisa decided she wanted to adopt me. At first, I felt loved, grateful that someone *finally* wanted to keep me. But then, I panicked. I ran, literally.

It was just months before my 18th birthday, and I stayed with a friend from school. I felt terrible about disappearing from the Jacksons' life, but in the end, they were probably better off without me. They'd forget about me, surely. Or so I'd thought.

Tragedy struck again, a few years later, when Lisa died of cancer. A lawyer for her estate contacted me one day while I was studying for my MBA, and 24 hours later, I learned she'd left me one-third of her estate. The rest was left to Rhonda. I looked up Rhonda online and told her she could have my portion. She refused, saying that her mother had wanted me to have it. Then she hung up. Of course, I eventually used the windfall to purchase the resort.

But one important thing happened in between. Terry *goddamn* Grant. Even though he hadn't responded to any of my messages after our summer fling when I was 19, I'd still held out hope. We had promised to meet in Shipsvold on Christmas Eve. Well, I should've known, but I was stupid and hopeful.

Of course, he didn't show up.

I couldn't do Christmas any more. I just couldn't. I tried, the first year after that. But I just oscillated between thinking about my Dad and thinking about Terry, both leading to stupid tears and feelings I didn't want to deal with. Sometimes anger. Sometimes depression. That was the last time I celebrated Christmas. I decided I didn't need the holiday anymore.

But I'm tired of letting the past dictate the present. I'm not going to let stupid Terry ruin Christmas for me—I never should have let him in the first place. I won't let him ruin what it means to me, the memories of Dad, and all the new memories I can make.

I *will* buy that Christmas village.

When Mariana Northam decides—when *I* decide to do something, I make it happen.

I will buy it, and I will make Dad proud.

Chapter 7

While nursing the hangover headache from hell, I wondered for a moment who had it worse, me or Jesse. But probably me, since he was probably used to drinking heavily. He was Jesse Cane, hard partying star. I was Mariana, and my middle name was Regret.

This was not how I wanted today to go. I'd gone to bed last night with so much determination, a will like I'd never had before. And I'd had plenty before. I'd risen from basically nothing, after all. Less than nothing, since I'd saddled myself with student loans at first. Of course, I'd had help along the way. I wouldn't be where I am today without the inheritance from Lisa Jackson, but when I bought the resort, it was struggling financially. I'd transformed it from nearly bankrupt to incredibly successful, and Northam Resort was now Northam Resorts. We had two other locations, and our ten-year plan included further expansion.

The Christmas village hadn't been in that plan, and I'd shocked my leadership team when I'd announced my intention. I didn't mind that—a bit of unpredictability keeps everyone on their toes. Let them wonder.

It was already past 9 am, and I was sitting in my office with my bathrobe on, sipping my second coffee between bites of buttery toast. I'd scrolled through the morning's work emails and found nothing urgent to attend to. Jesse Cane was already on his way to the airport, but Stacy Immers was leaving later today. I was relieved. The last thing I needed was for them to have a blowout at the airport that was later connected back to the resort. I had a great PR team, but they weren't as helpful outside of these walls.

As the caffeine and pain reliever began to kick in, my thoughts returned to my goal. I had to find a way to convince Jane. But how?

Jane seemed amenable to the sale when we'd met. Had Nina changed her mind? It was hard to believe, as Nina seemed so sweet. She reminded me of the grandmother I'd always wished I had.

Or did Terry have something to do with it? They seemed close.

It seemed possible, but … I didn't want to believe he'd sink that low. Would he?

But why? Why did he seem to resent me? If anyone should be resentful, it's me. He hurt me. Why does he think he has a reason to hate me?

I shook my head, unable to make sense of it.

Whatever the reason though, it seemed unavoidable. I had to talk to him. He obviously had Jane's ear, and if he could convince her not to sell, there's a good chance he could persuade her back in a more favorable direction too.

The idea of talking to him again made my stomach turn. Or maybe that was the hangover. But I saw no other option.

OK, with that decided, now how do I find him? I have no idea where he lives, no phone number. No idea where he hangs out. Asking Jane might look suspicious. All I know is he works at the shop, but I don't know his work schedule.

I frowned as I opened my laptop to look up the shop hours.

Wait, today is the day after Thanksgiving. Black Friday! Also known as the day that *every* person working in retail has to work.

My mouth curved into a smile. He has to be there today!
Oh wait, today the shop has extended hours.
Why didn't I think of that?
He could work morning, afternoon, or evening hours. Or

some combination. Should I call and ask what time he works today? No, that would sound like a stalker. And they probably can't give me that information anyway, unless I say I'm someone he knows.

Think, Mariana. Probably the least weird thing to do would be to just go there and pretend to shop while I look around for him. If he's not there, I can just … come back later. Or drive around and look for his car, which I remember seeing the other day.

Nope, too stalkerish, Mariana. I shook my head. It must be the hangover messing with my head still. I was never going to drink again.

Less than an hour later, I was bundled up in a winter coat and boots because it was snowing and freezing outside. The temperature in the shop was a bit stifling though even as I just started roaming around. Well, inching my way through it. There were so many people, it was hard to move. I'd rarely gone out shopping on Black Friday, at least not in the morning, so I wasn't used to the overwhelming crowds. At least I'd kept my shades on though, maintaining a facade of anonymity.

After what felt like forever, every imaginable body part was sweaty, and I felt like I'd never find him, even if he was here. But then out of the corner of my eye, I saw that dark head of hair lifting something from a high shelf. I breathed a sigh of relief and started making my way toward him, though progress was slow since I didn't want to knock over any displays or, well, people.

Finally, I reached him as he was stocking a shelf of candles. "Terry."

He glanced up, his arm pausing on the box in front of him, but only for a moment. He resumed stocking. "What?"

I bristled at his tone, but I kept mine courteous. "We need to talk."

"We do?" He continued placing candles on the shelf.

I bit my tongue to keep from saying something rude. "Yes. We … I need to talk to you."

He put two more candles on the shelf and then turned to me, looking me up and down. "I'm working. Can't you see that?"

"Well, yes, but I was hoping—"

"And it's Black Friday. We're really busy."

"I know, but maybe—"

He narrowed his eyes. "Mariana has come, so I should drop everything, right?"

My anger was rising, but I tried to keep a lid on it. "What are you talking about? I—"

"I have a job to do. I can't talk to you now." He gave me a dark look before resuming the candle stocking.

My heart racing, I thought about leaving. Stomping away, or maybe leaving with my nose in the air. But did I do that?

Nope.

"You … you jacka—jackanape!" Because even when I'm mad and basically yelling, I sound prissy, apparently.

His hand froze, and his head turned toward me. I kept going, unfazed. "I didn't mean we had to talk *right now.* Just, whenever. I didn't know how else to contact you, but to find you here. Which hasn't exactly been easy on the worst shopping day of the year." I paused for a moment to catch my breath, which was coming fast. "I don't know what your problem is with me. I'm not the one who—" A shadow crossed over his face.

"Ugh, never mind. I get it, you're working, and we can't talk. I will keep this short and sweet. Stay out of my business, Terry. Including my business with Jane. I don't know what you said to her, but you have messed up something really important to me, and now you need to fix it. Please, don't be a jerk."

His eyes were slightly wider than usual, and then they swept past me. I realized then that our surroundings seemed quieter.

Oh no. No, no, no.

I turned my head, with more reluctance than I'd ever felt with anything.

I knew what I'd see.

Yep, a rapt crowd had formed around us.

They'd heard every word.

I closed my eyes in mortification. "I—I'm sorry for the disturbance, everyone. Please … Happy Thanksgiving." I looked briefly back at Terry and then at the crowd, including another employee who'd walked over. "I'll be on my way out now."

Before I could escape though, Terry stood up quickly, leaned close, and whispered, "I'm on lunch break in 10 minutes. Wait outside."

I looked up into his dark eyes. He looked … not insincere. I nodded briefly and then darted out of the store. This time, my path was quick, as the crowd parted for me.

I stood as close to the building as I could, trying to avoid being snowed on, but the wind was foiling my attempt. Of course, I hadn't worn a hat today, so my hair was a drenched, tangled mess. I tried not to think of how horrible it looked; I never let anyone see me without my carefully straightened hair. But I'm sure my appearance wasn't nearly as destroyed as my dignity. I tried not to think about how many people had heard me inside, how much they had heard. Maybe no one recognized me, but … what if they did.

I shook my head, shivering. No, it seemed unlikely. My world at the resort didn't often mix with the world of the townsfolk.

But it would in the future. I couldn't be this careless again.

Through eyelids blanketed by snowflakes—my sunglasses abandoned—I stared out at the white landscape around me. Despite the weather, people were everywhere, as expected. And why wouldn't they be? This was one of the snowiest parts of the country. It was basically in our blood.

As my brain started to relax even as my body shook, I suddenly felt a pressure at my side.

"Walk with me," he simply said.

I looked up and to the left, but he was already moving. I scrambled to catch up, almost losing my footing on some slippery snow.

"Careful, princess," he warned. "I'm headed to lunch, just

over there."

"Oh, I'm not hungry. I just—"

He chuckled. "Well, good, because I wasn't inviting you to lunch. I'm just offering you a minute to talk while I walk over there. So talk."

I bristled at his sharp tone.

"I was hoping, uh … I mean, I wanted—"

"I work in lowly retail, my lady. We don't get long lunch breaks. So spit it out." He wasn't even looking at me, but I could hear his brisk tone clearly through the wind.

I inhaled deeply. The cold air was fortifying. "As I said in the shop, I need you to stop sabotaging me. With Jane."

He actually turned to look at me then, but he didn't slow his steps. "Oh, is that what I'm doing?"

"It would seem so. And I am pleading for you to stop. This business deal is important to me. Please don't ruin it." I hated begging but … if begging was required, begging is what I'd do.

We reached the sidewalk in front of the little cafe. He stopped and crossed his arms. "And why should I care?"

"Why should you …" I swallowed with some effort.

Don't cry, don't cry. Use your brain, not your emotions.

"I wouldn't dream of asking you to care about me. I know that's not in the cards." I heard the bitterness in my voice, but I kept going. "But what about the people of Shipsvold … and the visitors? I can take what Jane's built here and keep it alive, make it better, and by doing so, help this community by bringing in more tourist dollars and more festivities for the locals." I offered a gracious smile. "Everyone wins."

But he looked bored. "You mean *you* win. You haven't asked the *locals* what they want, have you?"

I opened my mouth to argue back, but I couldn't. He was right, I hadn't. But I could. "It'll be a part of our process during and after the sale. *If* there's a sale."

"And you think I'm standing in your way." His lips twisted into a slight smile at that, but it wasn't a friendly one.

My eyes narrowed to slits as I stepped a bit closer to him.

"Oh, I know you are. And it needs to stop. Right now. Or I'll—"

"Or what?" He licked his lips.

I scowled. Was this a game to him? Taunting me?

But before I could reply, I heard a feminine voice calling his name. We both turned to look, and a blonde woman was approaching.

He went to her immediately, throwing his arms around her.

Who was this woman? And why did her hair look perfect even in blowing snow? How did he know her? My stomach turned. It must have been the hangover nausea again. I stood there like an idiot, unsure whether our conversation was done—whether I wanted it to be.

Finally, she pulled away from him, laughing. "I'm starving, Terry," she said, tugging on his arm.

He turned, looking at me briefly before turning back to her. "Well, I was—"

I spoke up, hoping my voice sounded polite and not the mushy pile of insecurity that I was experiencing right now. "I'll leave you with your lunch date, Terry. Please consider my request."

"Mari—"

The woman stepped closer, eyeing me with curiosity. "Terry, do you know her?" As she took in my undoubtedly disheveled appearance, her expression morphed into one of disdain.

And I realized who she was.

Blair.

The corners of his mouth turned down. "I … used to know her. So did you. This is Mariana. We … well, she worked at the resort that summer before Mom and Dad passed."

Blair's eyes widened, whether at the memory of her parents' death or at the realization of who I was, I wasn't sure. Then, with a shrug, she said, "I'm not sure I remember."

"I remember you," I said. Oh, did I remember her. She didn't like me then, and it was clear she didn't like me now. But she had her brother wrapped around her finger, and he hadn't believed me back then when I'd told him she hated me. "She's just a little reserved sometimes," he had claimed. I'd given up trying to convince him. Instead of seeing her as the evil witch she was, he still looked up to his big sister. For whatever reason, she could do no wrong.

"How nice," Blair said, her tone polite, her eyes anything but.

"Mariana actually owns the resort now," he added. "Unlike us, she's done quite well for herself in the last decade." He said this with a slight laugh, but his sister didn't join him.

"Indeed, I wouldn't have thought …" I watched as her face changed again. She smiled brightly. "Well, we should have lunch sometime, Marian! Wouldn't it be so fun to catch up?"

"Sure," I said flatly. "And it's Mariana."

Yeah, that will never happen.

"Great!" She flashed her unnaturally white teeth at me and then at Terry. "Well, I'm starving, but uh, if you two …"

"Nope, we're done." He speared me with his dark brown eyes. "Aren't we?"

I swallowed, my breath coming a little faster. "Ya—yes. Thank you, Mr. Grant. Blair, it was nice to see you again." Before I could make a fool of myself any longer, I spun around quickly to exit the scene.

But stepping too fast on snowy ground is never a good idea, as I realized when I ended up on the ground, eating snow.

Just seconds later, I heard soft laughter in my ear. "Need a hand?"

"Go away," I growled. I could get up on my own.

"Fine." He laughed again this time as he stood back up. "Ms. Northam has got this. Come on, sis, let's go."

What a colossal failure of a day.

I wondered if I had any eggnog left.

Chapter 8

"I am so beyond tired."

I eyed my friend, who'd unceremoniously sunk into her soft couch. "I told you we could talk tomorrow."

Hazel tried to stifle a yawn. "You know what they say about jet lag. Go to bed at the usual time to adjust quickly …"

I frowned. I couldn't argue with that. For once, she was doing things properly, in that sense.

"Besides, you need my help."

Rolling my eyes, I grabbed one of the takeout containers on the couch and handed it to her. "You always think that."

"Well, you always do." She laughed. "Admit it, you can't live without me."

I bit back a smile. Considering how much I'd messed things up while she'd been in Japan, she might have a point. "I don't know how you could even help though. It's … he's so …"

"So … what?" She looked at me, taking a bite of her lo mein.

"I don't know," I said, looking down at my own food. "Stubborn. Among other things. Bull-headed, probably."

"Sounds familiar," she said with a giggle. "OK, so Terry is really stubborn, and you went down there and demanded he stop interfering. It's so shocking that didn't go over well. Especially while he was working."

I exhaled loudly. I'd told her the story on our way home from the airport after I'd picked her up, and I was already starting to regret having told her. "Yeah, well, what was I supposed to do? Beg?"

Hazel shrugged. "Maybe."

My jaw dropped, and I shook my head quickly. "Uh, no. Mariana doesn't beg."

She gave me a sideways glance. "It's weird when you do the third-person thing." She took another bite. "Maybe not beg exactly, but ... ask?"

"I did ask."

That's what I did. Was she not listening at all?

"I think you demanded. Not the same thing."

"Well, you weren't there—"

"No, but I know you, Mari."

I scowled. "Whose side are you on?"

She sighed, scooting closer to me on the couch and giving me a quick side hug before settling back on her side. "Yours, dummy. You know that. I think ... you don't realize sometimes how you come across."

I stiffened. "I'm very self-aware."

"I think you're aware of your own perception."

My brows furrowed as I considered what she was saying. Was it true?

She might have a point. Maybe.

"Fine, maybe I was too demanding. Maybe confronting him at work wasn't ideal. Now he'll never forgive me—is that what you're saying? This is all doomed to fail?"

She laughed. "Not at all. In fact, the dynamic shifted at the end, and that's to our advantage, I think." At my blank look, she added, "He got the last laugh. Literally."

"As in, watching me fall on my face in the snow? Yeah, thanks for that reminder. How the hell is that helpful?" I set my fried rice on the end table, too frustrated to eat.

"Because even if you were bossy or domineering earlier, the scene ended with you in a vulnerable position. He might've laughed, but I'll bet he also felt some empathy. And *that* we can work with."

"I didn't detect a trace of empathy, Hazel. Trust me, he just thought it was hilarious." And probably labeled me a klutz in his mind.

"Of course you didn't detect it, Mari. You weren't meant to. He's not the type to wear his heart on his sleeve." She took a sip of her drink and then mumbled, "Like someone else I know."

"I heard that," I said, but I smiled a bit. It was part of his appeal, I think. It *had been* part of his appeal. Nothing about him was appealing now. Well, except those lean lines of his face, that jaw and the rare smile, the hair that just begged to be tugged, the pecs that—

"What are you thinking about?" Hazel asked.

My eyes widened. "Nothing."

"Right." She arched an eyebrow and then shook her head. "So, I think you have to butter him up."

"*Butter* him up?" I asked, my voice rising. I tried to block out the inappropriate images that came to mind unbidden.

Crap. What was happening to me?

I felt my cheeks redden and some other uncomfortable heat throughout my body.

Hazel was peering at me, the corners of her mouth turned up slightly. "Yes. You know, be nice to him. Catching flies with honey."

"Oh," I croaked. "I see—that's … I don't know if I can do that." I cleared my throat.

She tilted her head. "Are you all right, Mari?"

"I'm fine," I said, too quickly. I took a steadying breath. "I just don't know if I'm capable of being nice to *him*. He doesn't deserve it." Yes, remember that. He doesn't deserve any of my thoughts, certainly not sexy ones. I needed to rein this in *now*.

"Really? I've known you for years, Mari, and I've seen you be polite and kind to some of the most awful human beings over the years. Rich prigs who would sell their mother to make a profit. Well, maybe not nice exactly—you don't tolerate bad behavior—but polite at least. You've dealt with much worse than Terry Grand."

"Grant," I mumbled.

"What?"

"It's—never mind. I guess you're right."

She wasn't right though. All those other jerks were just jerks that I'd never cared about. But Terry … we had a past. And it needed to stay in the past.

"I don't think you understand what you're asking me to do, Haz," I said, running a hand over my face.

She peered at me closely. "Maybe I don't." After a long pause, she asked softly, "Do you still have feelings for him?"

Panic coursed through me. I felt my palms get sweaty as my heart rate soared. I'm certain my face looked like a tomato. "No, that's crazy," I said emphatically. I sat up straighter, willing my body to cooperate with my authoritative tone. "I'm not a romantic sap, like you." And she was too, despite her usually casual attitude toward relationships. "In fact, I might even be aromantic."

"I had a friend in college who was aro. They were nothing like you. And they certainly hadn't had a love story that haunted them for years. That seems kinda like the opposite of aro."

"I'm not *haunted* by this … not even a love story. A fling. You've got it all wrong," I insisted, looking away.

"Maybe. But you said I'm a romantic sap, and I say, well, it takes one to know one." Her foot nudged me then. When I looked up, she smiled. "Oh, Mari. Lighten up."

I stared at my lap for a while. "So, what should I do?"

She grinned, tucking her legs under her as she turned more fully toward me. "You have to win over Jane, right? So if Terry's the obstacle, you need to win him over." When I balked at this, she gave me a sympathetic smile. "I'm not saying you have to date him, or even befriend him. Just … try a gentler approach. Maybe let down your guard a little."

I tried not to react as I looked away again. She had me until "let down your guard"—I never did that anymore, and I certainly wouldn't do it with him. Not again.

When my eyes swung back to her face, she had a knowing smile but didn't say anything for a long moment. "So, let's see, we'll need to find a way for you to spend some time together a little more casually, where he can be a little more relaxed, not around his work. Maybe even something fun, to get some endorphins on our side."

As her face took on a thoughtful expression, mine was balking. "That sounds ... hard. He'll see right through it. It's not at all something I'd do—especially with the way our interactions have been."

She seemed not to hear me, staring into space for a long moment. Then her eyes lit up. "I know! The annual Winter Wonderland event this weekend. It's perfect. Fresh air, lots of fun things to do, a different environment where you can talk or even just shoot the breeze—"

I winced. "Hazel, do I look like someone who shoots the breeze?"

She laughed, almost to the point of tears. "Point taken. But hear me out. This is happening on the lake, just outside the Christmas village and, of course, adjacent to the resort. It would offer a really natural way for you to bring up some of your ideas for what to do with the village if you can buy it."

She looked so damn excited that I tried to think about what she was saying. "I guess that is a good point. But isn't Jane the one I need to convince of that? Not Terry."

"You need to convince them both, obviously. But we already talked about this—you need to deal with the Terry obstacle first, if he's really that much of an influence over her. And that's a big 'if,' but it's all we have to go on at this point." She flipped her ponytail over her shoulder and paused. "I guess you could always invite them both, if you want."

"Hmm. What if I end up being this awkward third wheel though? I mean, it seems like they're close, and neither of them like me. They'll probably just ditch me and go enjoy themselves."

Hazel nodded. "It's possible. I don't want to agree that they dislike you ... who could dislike you? You're a wonderful person, Mari. But still ..."

"You could come," I offered. *Please come*, I thought. "In fact,

I don't think I can do it without you." Oh, no. Did I really just admit that aloud? Where is my dignity these days? I haven't even had a drop of alcohol today. I lowered my head in shame.

"I can't …" she trailed off. "I can't wait. This will be so fun! Well, if they say yes."

My eyes swung up to hers, gratitude pouring out of me. I knew she'd been about to say no. She was simply the best. "I can't thank you enough."

"Oh, sure you can." She laughed. "We'll be watching *Love in the Time of Yoga* tonight. That's how you'll repay me, even if you loathe every moment, mu-hahaha."

"Ah, joke's on you then. I already watched it over the holiday last week. I don't mind seeing it again. But I thought you were *so* tired?" I grinned.

"Wait, *what*? You watched a rom-com without me? Without coercion?" Her eyes were as huge as I'd ever seen them. "What's gotten into you?" Then a massive smile overtook her face. "OK, you're officially a romantic sap too. I declare it."

I tried not to laugh but failed. "And you're officially annoying." When we stopped laughing, I leaned back onto the couch cushions. "Back to this weekend though, Haz, how the heck are we going to invite them to the Winter Wonderland event without being super awkward?"

"Oh, it'll be awkward. There's no way around that. But that's OK." She bit her lip, picking up her phone. "Let's find out all the details first and then figure out how to ask them."

"You said this is annual? How do you know?"

"Oh, I went with Ryan last year. That guy with the … never mind. I think the year before, Caitlyn and I went." She looked up from her phone. "You've never gone?"

I shook my head.

I didn't even know it existed. I suppose I knew that some festivals or events happened in the winter around here, but I hadn't paid much attention to it. My life has been so isolated to the resort happenings, so focused on work and nothing else. I not only worked but *lived* here too, despite Hazel's frequent nagging to find a place of my own.

Guilt coursed through me—who was I to intrude upon this town and try to take over one of their best assets?

Chapter 9

My boots crunched in the snow as I took tentative steps toward the pavilion where we were meeting Jane and Terry.

"It's going to be fine," Hazel said, leaning in.

"Easy for you to say," I muttered.

"It is easy for me, because I have faith in you."

I tried to smile. "Thanks. I'm trying to—oh, I see them."

"They brought Nina." Hazel grinned at me. "That's probably a good thing. We need to win her over too."

I shrugged. I wasn't worried about Nina. She'd seemed pretty friendly and open to our proposal. I didn't think she would stand in our way. No, that obstacle was named Terry. And maybe a bit of Jane herself, with her capricious nature.

As we approached them, I took a steadying breath and arranged my expression in a warm smile. "Hello, Jane, Nina, wonderful to see you again. And Terry, you too." I tried not to make the last few words sound forced, though they definitely were.

He stood there with arms crossed over his well-defined chest and just nodded, his expression guarded.

"Well, the old lady and I were already planning to go," Jane said, nodding her head toward Nina. "She said we might as well let you girls tag along."

My smile faltered but only briefly. "Well, thank you." I took a deep breath and then exhaled, my breath visible in front of me. "I was hoping to have a chance to talk about some of my ideas for the village—" I stopped when I felt Hazel's hand on my shoulder.

"You know, since it sits so beautifully next to the annual festival here. But it's way too early for shop talk, am I right?" She smiled at the three of them. "Let's go have some fun. Where should we start? The sculpture contest entries are always fun to look at. I am *terrible* on skates, but I love watching others. Oh, and I remember last year's hot cocoa sold out early because it was so delicious!"

Nina nodded. "I remember it. I think they put caramel in it. You can't go wrong with adding caramel to, well, anything."

Well, she's not wrong. Caramel might be the best thing ever invented. Or discovered.

"So true." Hazel nodded. With that, she linked arms with both women and led them in the direction of the hot cocoa and coffee tent, leaving me to follow awkwardly … with Terry.

Had she done this on purpose?

Probably.

I took a fortifying breath. "So, Terry." The feel of his name on my tongue was still strange, and I felt it everywhere. "How are you?"

He fell into step beside me, albeit with what seemed like reluctance. "I'm fine. You?"

"I'm fine."

Now what do I say? Think, Mari. "Uh, it's nice that you have the day off work."

"I don't. I'm on the evening shift. Extended holiday hours." His tone was flat. My conversation wasn't impressing him. And why should it? I wasn't excelling at this.

"Oh, sorry to hear that," I said, trying to convey sympathy.

"It's not a bad thing. More hours at the shop equals more money."

I winced. How well I knew that, but it had been years since I'd worked an hourly wage or punched a time clock. "Yeah, sorry, I wasn't thinking."

"It's OK. When you're not used to struggling for money, you don't think that way. I get it. You are doing well for yourself, right?" He glanced at me and then looked forward again.

"I … yes. But I wasn't always. I'm sure you know that. I worked more hourly jobs than you can imagine." I took a breath, vowing to stop using a defensive tone. "Anyway, well, I … we're glad you had time to come out here with us today."

He looked at me a little longer and then laughed. "How much pride did you have to swallow to utter those words?"

My jaw dropped, but before I could respond, he added, "You can deny it if you'd like, but it'll just give me more to laugh about."

My brows furrowed, and then I looked over at him. "I won't deny it then."

He didn't quite smile, but he wasn't frowning either. OK, I could work with that.

"Do you—"

"I wondered—"

We both stopped.

"You first," he said.

"Uh, I …" What was I going to say? I was blanking. Completely blank. Hurry, think of something. "Do you like winter?"

Well, that's going to move him to change his mind. Pathetic. I used to be good at conversation, when I had to be. I tried not to cringe visibly.

He stole a quick glance at me before looking around. "I do. I find the cold invigorating. Winter sports are fun." He looked at me again. "How about you? I got the sense at that party that you like Christmas but definitely not Halloween, so at least you like winter holidays."

He remembered that detail from the party. But did he not remember all those years ago, when we were supposed to meet at Christmas? I tried not to show the anguish on my face and looked away for a moment. "I do like winter holidays, but I'm more of a spring and summer person."

We made eye contact for a bit longer than was comfortable, and I had to look away. "So, uh, it's not too cold today."

"Nah, it's just right," he said. Was that boredom in his tone? Probably. It's like all my conversation skills abandoned me today.

"Chilly enough so the snow sculptures aren't melting, but not so cold that we're all miserable, you know?" I heard myself saying.

"Yeah." After a beat, he looked at me. "We don't have to talk, you know. We can just walk. I know it's a slow walk with two old ladies in the snow, but we're almost there."

I scoffed. "I know we don't *have* to talk." I swallowed a huge helping of pride again. "I just … just wanted to."

His expression was curious as he opened his mouth to reply, but Jane's commanding voice cut through our bubble. "Where's that boy? Terry, can you hold this purse? It weighs more than I do, and I need my hands free."

He stepped forward, taking the purse, and within a minute we'd reached the line for hot drinks. I groaned when I saw how long it was, but Jane simply walked up to the front, waving to the barista. Hazel and I looked at each other in confusion but followed them.

Jane turned back to look at us approaching. "Well, hurry up. We don't have all day to wait for the young folks. Tell Eleanor what you want."

I looked at Nina and then at Terry, who nodded slightly. OK, I guess Jane was special and got to skip the line. We quickly gave our drink orders, and Terry ushered the ladies over to a table to wait.

"How do you think it's going, Mari?" she asked. "You and Terry didn't look like you were fighting, at least."

I chuckled. "No, not fighting. But I wouldn't say it's gone great. I'm just not good at this. I don't know what I'm doing. Let's try to stay together so I'm not responsible for making awkward conversation, OK? You have a million times more charm than I do."

Hazel laughed. "I'll do my best. You sell yourself short.

You're probably just nervous. This wouldn't be easy for anyone, you know. If it's easy for me, that's because he's not my ex."

I nodded slowly. She had a point. Still, I had higher expectations for myself.

Once the drinks were made, we brought them over to the table and sat down. Conversation was easy for a while, with Hazel and Nina keeping things light and even funny. The moody Jane even chuckled a couple times, and I also saw Terry crack a smile, which then vanished when he caught me watching him. Sigh.

After a while, I asked the group, "So, what should we do next? Should we go look at the ice sculptures, explore the ice cave, watch the children's skit, or—"

"They're snow sculptures, not ice sculptures, my dear," Jane corrected me.

"Oh, sorry." I was always getting things wrong. I wanted to cry, but instead I pasted an excited smile on my face. "Even better! Should we go do that now?"

"I was thinking I'd love to go watch the ice skaters. I heard the local skating club is out there today. They're actually pretty good. Have you girls seen them perform?" Nina asked us.

Wow, I really hadn't done anything in this town. Before I could own up to my shame though, Hazel jumped in. "Not yet, but I've been dying to! I love watching ice skating. Mariana, you're actually pretty good on skates yourself, aren't you? I remember you skated in college."

A warning sounded in my brain. This conversation could easily go south. "Ah, I did, but that was years ago. I'm sure I've already forgotten how." It wasn't true—I went skating every year in a small frozen lake in the woods behind the resort, but Hazel probably didn't know that.

"Terry is an excellent skater," Jane said, smiling at Terry. Of course only *he* would get her rare smiles. "He played ice hockey in high school, didn't he, Nina?"

"Oh yes, he was and still is a great skater. Hey, I bet he could help you relearn, Mariana."

Panic surged through me. "Oh, I doubt—"

"She wouldn't want to skate with me," he said, his eyes trained on me.

My heart raced, and I knew I was trapped. Refuse, and I looked terrible in front of Jane and Nina. Accept and … well, skate with Terry. Potentially even touch him.

Would I survive that?

What was the worst-case scenario here?

I don't know. I felt frozen with indecision.

But they were all looking at me. I had to decide.

"I guess she doesn't want to," Jane said, pursing her lips. "Her loss."

I could barely breathe, but I managed to get out, "Wait, yes, I do. Sorry, I was just … I had a bad fall once and was thinking about that for a moment. I'll put it out of my mind."

Big lie. But it would do.

Nina looked at me with sympathy, and Jane looked mollified.

Terry's eyes were narrowed though. "All right then. The rest of you can go find a place to watch, if you'd like." He stood up and held out his hand to me. "You. Let's go rent some skates."

I was supposed to take his hand? Oh, I was well and truly screwed.

*****

Should I tell him I already know how to skate? I didn't know if it was better to admit I'd lied about being out of practice or to stick to the lie but have to endure his teaching me and possibly touching me while he "helped" me. These thoughts plagued me as we put our skates on.

Then again, Jane may be out there watching. She'll probably expect me to look like I don't know how to skate, at least at first. I suppose I'd better act like I don't know what I'm doing.

"So have you really not been out on the ice at all, or just not very often?" he asked as we reached the ice.

"Um." I stepped onto the ice, gliding out a bit and then making myself wobble a bit. He grabbed my hand then.

Thank goodness we had gloves on. I couldn't have handled skin-on-skin contact right now.

Why, I don't want to think about. It's not like I want him. I don't even like him. I hate him, I think.

But even through the glove, I could feel the muscles in his hands flexing and intertwining with mine, and I became lost in the sensation ... and I fell. Without even trying.

"Woah, I got you," he said, strengthening his grip on my hand while kneeling down.

My knee had almost slammed into the ice, but not quite—he'd broken my fall. I looked up with reluctant gratitude. "Thank you."

I continued to feel shaky while skating hand in hand with him, so distracted I was by his touch, his nearness. I sighed. "Let me try it on my own," I said, looking at him with pleading eyes.

His eyes swung to mine, doubt written all over his face. "Really? I don't mind holding on, if that's what you're worried about."

"No, it's—thank you. I just want to try." I can't just say *I'll do a thousand times better if I'm not distracted by you being so close.* "If I fall on my face, I'll come running back to you, OK?" I gave him a small smile.

He shrugged, letting go of my hand slowly. "Your call. I won't be far away."

I started slow and eventually gathered some speed. Soon I was flying across the ice, the wind in my face. This was the first time I'd been skating this year, and it felt glorious.

For a moment, I forgot about Terry. And it took him a moment to catch up, probably because he'd been caught off guard by my speed. But he did catch me, calling out, "Dark horse!"

I grinned and started skating backward, and he followed my lead as we circled the rink a few times. Belatedly I noticed

Jane, Nina, and Hazel waving on the edge of the rink, and I called to Terry to let him know.

We skated over to them.

"That was crazy to watch," Hazel said. "I was thinking, either Terry is an amazing teacher, or you two have skated together before."

Terry chuckled, leaning on a post nearby. "Neither. She was a little rusty at first but then, well, you saw." I'd almost swear his look hinted at admiration.

I was probably blushing, but the cold weather would make my cheeks rosy regardless, so it was fine. "He did save me from a few nasty falls."

"You did make a nice pair," Jane declared. "But just sitting around is making me cold. We're going to get moving on to some of the other activities. You two can finish up and meet us at the sculptures."

"Or they could keep skating if they'd like to." Nina offered with a smile. "We'd be fine with Hazel."

"Oh, I don't want to miss out on any of the other activities," I said quickly. "Terry and I can finish up and join you soon."

Jane nodded. "Good. I need Terry for the sculpture viewing."

I looked to him in question, but his expression was blank.

We skated over to the other side where the warming hut was, not talking at all.

After removing our skates and putting our boots back on, we returned our skates to the rental booth.

"That was fun," I said, aiming for some more friendly conversation as we started the long path around the rink to where the other activities were occurring.

"I'm glad you enjoyed it."

What was that supposed to mean? "Didn't you?" I tried not to sound too defensive.

"Sure," he said, running a hand over his jaw.

"What does that mean?"

He looked at me with a strange expression then. "It means yes."

"Well, I know 'sure' means yes, but—"

And then I was down. Face first in the snow.

Something had fallen on my side though.

I turned my head, unable to fully move my upper body. I winced, feeling a slight ache.

Terry's body was half covering my own, braced slightly by one gloved hand. My eyes widened, snowflakes blurring my vision slightly.

"Sorry, I tried to catch you, but … well, you can see I didn't," he said, his lips twitching. He hadn't face planted into the snow, but one side of him was covered in snow.

"No, instead you landed on top of me. Thanks for that," I said with a glare, trying to suggest with my eyes that he move. But he didn't.

"What's up with you, Mariana? I don't remember you being clumsy. But you are always falling down."

"It's … I don't usually."

"Oh, so it's just around me?" Something glinted in his eyes. "Do I make you nervous?"

I was suddenly aware of my shortness of breath, from being in this awkward physical position and from this conversation. "I … no? I mean, no."

He stared at me for a long moment. "You have … you have snow on your face. Let me help you sit up." He slid off me, to the side, and then pulled me up by the arms. We were sitting close now, and he pulled the warm, dry part of his scarf from within his jacket and started using it to gently wipe my face.

Finally his movements slowed and eventually stopped. "There," he said, his voice almost a whisper. "All better."

I swallowed with some effort, my eyes bouncing between his. Memorizing every detail of his face, which I knew I'd never see again this close. I didn't even want to, I reminded myself.

Then I saw his eyes drop, and I knew he was looking at my lips. Before I could tell myself I absolutely shouldn't do the same, my eyes darted to his full lips, which were slightly parted and dark pink from the cold.

Without thinking, I licked my lips a little. I think he leaned in ever so slightly, but it might have been me.

Words were hard, and my body didn't want to produce any. But I managed to say, "Terry." At least I think so—some kind of vocal word-like sound.

He blinked a few times and then inhaled sharply, turning his head. After a long moment, he began to move away. When he looked back at me, he asked, "You're not hurt, are you?"

"No," I said, my voice hoarse. I coughed a bit to clear my throat. "A few more bruises won't kill me." I laughed, trying to lighten the mood. "Uh, thank you."

"Welcome," he muttered, offering me a hand to stand up, but I ignored it to get up on my own.

What had just happened? *Almost* happened?

Had we almost just kissed?

Or was I imagining it?

Oh my god, what if I had almost just kissed *him* and he wasn't interested at all?

Regardless, what a massive mistake that would've been.

Thank goodness he stopped it.

I should've stopped it though. Oh, why didn't I stop it? Why have I suddenly been having all these physical feelings around him? I don't like him, so I can't lust after him, can I?

I had no answers, but I knew one thing with certainty. This could never, ever happen again.

Chapter 10

I looked in my rearview mirror for the third time, making sure I didn't have any crumbs on my face or food between my teeth. I'd stress eaten the entire five-minute drive to the shop, which wouldn't seem like much time, but let's just say I'd finished off more cookies than I'd ever admit to.

I wasn't proud.

But damn, they were delicious.

Hazel had spent the morning with me cutting out, baking, and frosting these amazing Christmas cookies that I was about to deliver.

Unfortunately, I was left to deliver the cookies solo, as she had a business meeting in Minneapolis early tomorrow morning, and with the recent snow, she wanted to leave early and spend the night.

So, yeah. I was going to show up, unannounced, yet again, at Terry's place of work. Jane's too, because Hazel had said they would both be working—apparently she'd managed to gather a substantial amount of info from Jane yesterday when I'd been off nearly making a huge mistake in the snow.

At least this time though, I was delivering delicious treats, and I was hoping that would make them hate me less. Even a bit less. That would be a win, right? I'd take anything at this point. I was showing up near closing time so it would seem like rewarding the shop staff, and who knows, maybe Jane and Terry would be free to talk a bit afterward. I never really got a chance to talk to Jane about my ideas yesterday during the festival; by the time I finally had a chance, she'd pleaded tiredness and asked to go home.

With not a little trepidation, I parked my car, quite a distance from the shop front, since it was busy season. After retrieving the small suitcase full of goodies from the car, I made my way slowly to the front door. The last thing I needed was another embarrassing fall and awkward bruise.

Reaching the door, I took a deep breath, telling myself it would be fine. People love cookies. Even I couldn't bungle this, could I? As I was about to grab the door handle though, balancing the suitcase in my other arm, some customers opened the door fast. It was either me or the cookies, and I chose to save the cookies.

So there I was, on the ground again. Ouch. But the cookies were in my lap, safe. One of the customers was kind enough to apologize and help me up, and when I turned to go inside, that's when I saw it.

A full-on smile. Was he laughing? Or trying not to? I don't know, but that smile …

I could die happy, just having seen that smile this one last time. *That* smile, the smile to end all smiles, on *that* man. I couldn't think straight. I nearly dropped the cookies, and the customer who was holding the door cleared their throat.

The sound startled me, and I mumbled an apology as I tore my eyes away from him.

What was wrong with me? Why was I reacting to him this way? Was it the fall—did I hit my head? I thought it was only my butt and hand that hit the ground, but maybe I had a head injury somehow. I was walking through the door and looking down at my cookie suitcase when suddenly Jane's tinny voice was right there.

I looked up and pasted a smile on my face. "Jane! It's nice to see you again."

"Hello, Mariana," she said, her voice wary as she looked at my suitcase that I was holding awkwardly. "Have you some strange idea of moving in?"

I chuckled. The lady could be quite funny sometimes, I'll give her that. "Actually, I brought a little treat for everyone at the shop. I just thought it'd be easier to carry them in the suitcase."

Jane lifted one thin eyebrow. "A treat? For the shop?"

"Yes, I brought Christmas cookies." At her blank look, my smile wavered, but I continued, "I thought everyone's probably had a long weekend and deserved a nice treat."

Jane nodded slowly. "Well, that is true. Are they any good?"

I almost laughed. I was still getting used to her directness. "They're amazing. Hazel helped me make them, actually. Can I put them out somewhere for everyone to take from?"

Jane slowly lifted a finger to point to the register area. "That'll do. Well, I have work to do."

"Of course, Jane. Don't let me keep you," I said, smiling brightly.

"I won't," she said, raising her eyebrow. Then, in a softer tone, she added, "Thank you."

My smile was completely genuine then. This was a win. She'd thanked me! And she hadn't kicked me out immediately. This was progress.

But my happiness was short-lived, as I turned and saw Terry frowning from the other side of the main shop room. He seemed to be frowning in my direction. And then he turned to talk to someone and laughed. I saw his smile again ... but not toward me.

He was talking to the cashier, Cynthia. Only now, they weren't talking. He was hugging her.

He was doing what?

Why were they embracing?

And why was he smiling at her?

I looked away and tried to calm my racing pulse.

It was completely ridiculous for me to be having jealous thoughts. So maybe they were close ... friends? Or even if it were more, why would it matter? I'm over him, have been for so many years. As if I need another thing to worry about.

I snuck another glance, but both of them were out of view now, as a group of employees were moving a Christmas tree near where I was standing. It was then I realized I was still holding the cookie suitcase. I sighed.

Stop being so awkward and obsessive, and do what you came to do, Mari.

I ambled over to the register and opened the suitcase. As I started to arrange the cookies onto holiday-themed trays I'd brought, a deep voice reverberated in my ear.

"You again."

He was so close I could smell him, a faint scent of cologne or aftershave I'd noticed yesterday. Well, tried not to notice.

I took a slow breath and willed my stupid racing heart to settle down. Then, looking over my shoulder, I gave my best attempt at a friendly, platonic smile. "I'm afraid so. But I have something to sweeten the deal this time."

His eyebrows rose. "You think you can win us over with cookies?"

Oh, no. I shouldn't have led with that. Or said it at all. Probably.

"Oh, I—no, I didn't mean that literally. Just … figuratively, maybe a dose of sugar will make it easier to tolerate my presence."

I tried not to cringe, but damn, my usual eloquence has vanished lately.

His lips twitched. "I'll have to have a taste."

His intense, nearly black eyes stayed on mine as he leaned in slowly.

Oh my god, did he mean a taste of … the cookie, right? Or … I swallowed, unable to look away or move away.

But his arm had reached around me and grabbed a Santa cookie off the tray.

He stood straight again, and I stepped back a bit, putting some necessary space between us.

"Nice decorating. Did you make these?"

I was staring at the floor, unable to make eye contact after the foolish thoughts I was just having. I mean, seriously, what the hell was I thinking? I was going to lose this deal because I couldn't keep my emotions and crazy thoughts in check. But I was usually so good at that—I was Mariana Northam, after all. "Yeah."

He took a tiny bite. "OK, I haven't keeled over yet. So if they're poisoned, it's a slower-acting one, right?"

My eyes flew to his, but I saw that he didn't actually look afraid. He appeared to be laughing at me silently. I made a face at him. Because apparently I'm pretty immature now.

After taking a larger bite, he closed his eyes in an expression of bliss. "*Ahhh*. Now that's a Christmas cookie. You sure you made these?"

I crossed my arms. "I did." I didn't want to admit the rest, not to *him*, but I suppose I had to be honest. "With Hazel."

A knowing expression came over his face. "Ah. Well, they are delicious, Mariana. You can add baking to your many talents, I guess."

One of my eyebrows rose. "My many talents?"

"You always surprise me."

His admission caught me off guard because, well, it sounded sincere. And I think he meant it in a good way? I didn't know what to do with that.

"Well, uh, so … how was work today?"

I should collect my prize for the worst conversationalist ever. Somehow I used to be good at this. At least I think I was.

His eyes swung from the cookie tray and back to me. He grabbed another cookie and took his time chewing before answering my question. "Busy."

"Right, one would expect that on a Sunday only a few weeks before the Christmas holiday, I suppose."

"Yes, *one would*," he said with a smirk.

I narrowed my eyes. "Are you mocking my speech?"

His tongue in his cheek, he paused for a moment. "No. Maybe." He stared at me for a long time thoughtfully, as if unsure whether to continue. "You're different now, Mariana, even the way you talk."

My breath hitched. "Oh, I—what do you mean?"

He shook his head, a look of confusion on his face. "In some ways … I hardly recognize the girl I knew."

I averted my eyes. Well, that was the goal, wasn't it? I wanted to leave the old Mariana behind. Why did I get the feeling he saw it as a negative though?

"Is that a bad thing? We all change, don't we? Isn't that … good?"

Our eyes met, and I knew whatever he was going to say next was going to change things. Maybe between us or maybe just within myself. For some reason, I needed to know his answer like I needed to breathe—

"Terry, are you hogging all of Mariana's cookies?" Jane's voice cut through the haze of feelings, of need. I looked at her, standing beside us now, and I put a hand over my chest to still my breathing.

He looked at me for another beat, from my eyes, down to my hand on my chest, and then looked at Jane. "You know me too well, Janie. I suppose we should tell everyone else, right? Before I go into a diabetic coma from eating so many?"

I turned to him in horror, my heart beating a staccato rhythm all over again as I started to reach frantically for the cookie in his hand.

He held it over his head though and laughed. "Joking, of course. I may be an idiot sometimes, but not that much."

It took everything within me to fight the urge to glare at him at that point. He had spent the whole evening playing with my emotions, and this took the cake. Or the cookie, I suppose.

Jane went around the other side of the counter and retrieved a bell, which she pressed several times.

"Everyone! Please come to the main register," Terry shouted. Then he said it again, loudly but not shouting this time.

He really had a lovely voice even when he spoke overly loudly. Well, *lovely* wasn't the right word. More like *rich, deep, strong … sexy.*

I really needed to stop these pointless thoughts. Who cared about his damn voice? Not me.

As people started gathering around, I asked Jane if I could speak to the employees. She looked at Terry first, who shrugged. Then she nodded her acceptance.

"Hi everyone, I'm Mariana Northam. I run the resort 'round the lake, and I was hoping to get to know everyone in the Village a bit better." I looked around, and I mostly saw blank stares or bored expressions. I smiled and kept going. "So, I know you've had a busy work day, and all you want to do is go and enjoy your evening, so I won't keep you long. Just wanted to say hi and offer some Christmas cookies to enjoy on your way out tonight. Terry and Jane like them, and they're not easy judges." One or two quiet laughs. I smiled brighter. "Take one or two or a handful. I've got dozens, so you can seriously even take some for your dog if you want to." At this, more than a few people laughed or smiled, and I stepped out of the way so people could get to the cookie trays.

I followed Jane around to the other side of the register. "Jane, thanks for letting me talk to your employees and bring treats. It means a lot."

She looked at me for a moment and then nodded. "We're not going to say no to sweet treats around here." She paused before adding, "We have a room for nursing mothers. But currently no nursing mothers work here."

My eyes scrunched together in complete confusion. Did she have me confused with someone else? "Oh, um, I don't have a baby."

She raised an eyebrow. "Do I look like I was born yesterday? Obviously you're not a mother." She scoffed. "I mean if you want some rest for that ankle for a bit. There aren't a lot of comfortable, quiet places to sit down out here or in the back."

My eyes widened. "Oh, how did you know about my ankle—"

"Again, sweetie, not born yesterday. You've been limping, and I saw you ice skating. Terry said you've taken a few falls."

Oh he did, did he? I wonder what all he'd told her. Surely not about the part after the last fall—*oh, shut up, Mariana, stop thinking about that!*

"Jane, truly, thank you so much. This is so thoughtful. I'll take you up on that offer." I smiled at her and patted her on the upper arm. "If I don't see you again this evening, I hope you have a nice one and that I can see you again soon."

She nodded, not smiling but not frowning either. I'll take that.

Some time later, maybe five minutes or twenty, I heard a sharp knock on the door. I opened my eyes slowly. I'd been relaxing in the comfy chair and nearly fallen asleep.

Me, relaxing. It wasn't something I did often.

But something about this room, I mean, wow. There was calming music, soft lighting, and Zen decor. I didn't usually go for that sort of thing, but I loved this. I could live for this.

But yeah, someone was knocking. I wanted to shout, "Go away!" And I should have. Because it was the last person I wanted to see. The person most likely in the world to destroy my calm.

In walked Terry, and without even asking if I minded the company, he sat down in the extra chair in the room. I wondered why there was another chair in the room. Would two nursing mothers want to nurse together? I had no idea, as I knew nothing about nursing. Or parenting. Maybe some day, but my life wasn't going in that direction, and I probably wouldn't make a good mother anyway. I frowned, thinking about this. Maybe this would be the only time I'd ever spend in a nursing mothers' room. I wasn't sure how to feel about that, but I felt a dull jab in my chest area.

Terry cleared his throat, jarring me from the mental haze I was in.

Reluctantly, I sat up straighter and then cleared my own throat, as it felt kind of scratchy. "If you're wondering why I'm here, Jane told me I could rest here. I'm not, like … squatting here or something." I sighed. "But I'm also not a nursing mother."

Why I added that last bit, I have no idea, but I regretted it immediately after saying it. It sounded too personal, between us, now basically strangers.

He was quiet for a long, long time, his elbows resting on his knees. He wasn't looking at me.

Finally, his gaze met mine, and he spoke. "What are you doing here?"

Something about his quiet, steady voice was unnerving. I felt a little chill run through me, and I think it was nerves, but … I wasn't sure. I tried to maintain eye contact.

But I failed. "I-I-I told you—"

"I know why you brought the damn cookies, Mariana," he said, his eyes flaring with frustration.

My eyes flew to his. "Then why did you—"

"Why are you *here*, in this room?"

"Well, Jane noticed I was limping," I said with a sheepish smile. "She was right. I was a bit sore from yesterday. So I'm just resting."

He narrowed his eyes. "But why not go home and do that?"

Dammit.

Why *didn't* I?

I furrowed my brow, not even sure how to answer. I couldn't meet his eyes. Somehow I knew whatever answer I came up with wouldn't satisfy him. I didn't even know the goddamn answer myself. Did I?

"Don't give me some B.S. answer, Mariana," he warned.

Given his harsh tone, I looked up quickly and saw that his jaw muscles were tight. He was angry. Or at least annoyed.

And I was feeling too many things.

Confused.

Nervous.

Regretful.

Intrigued.

Wait, what? No, just no.

Embarrassed?

Why, I'd done nothing wrong.

But I felt like he'd caught me, somehow. Seen through me. I didn't like feeling this vulnerable, this …

Invigorated.

Shaking my head to try to clear my thoughts and damnable feelings, I did my best to look him in the eye with what little remained of my dignity. "Well, it was kind of Jane to offer, so I thought it only kind to accept." Well, that was a dumb reason if I'd ever heard one. "Besides, after the cookies were eaten, I'd need my trays back."

"Both great reasons to be sitting in the nursing mothers room at my place of work," he said sarcastically.

Well, I couldn't disagree with his sarcasm there. I wasn't great at thinking on my feet around him. Or thinking of any kind.

After another long, awkward silence, he stood up suddenly with a huff and started pacing for a minute or so. I just sat there for a bit and then asked, "Terry? Everything OK?"

He ignored me but sat back down. After just a bit more glaring at the floor, he broke the silence. In more ways than one.

"Could you *be* any more transparent, Mariana?"

My heart jumped into my throat as I watched his eyes flare with resentment. "I'm not, uh, not sure what you mean—" I started to say, barely audible.

"Cut the crap." He said, his jaw clenched. "I can save us both a lot of trouble and tell you it's not going to work."

I flinched, and I opened my mouth to speak but couldn't form a sentence. "What … you … is this—" What was he referring to? Did he think I was trying to seduce him, or worse? How mortifying—I had to eliminate this idea from his mind right away. I swallowed and smoothed my hair, trying to summon the cool, sophisticated Mariana. I thought of what he'd done, all those years ago.

That did the trick.

"You'll have to be more specific," I managed to say, my voice relatively unaffected.

His lips pressed into a thin line, and he shook his head as

he looked past me for a moment. Then, his angry stare returned to me, stronger than ever. "I know you can't stand me. You're using me to get to her."

I gasped. How the hell was I supposed to respond to that? I couldn't argue with the fact that I didn't like him. I certainly couldn't say that I *do* like him. And, well, the fact that I was using him—well, of course I was. That was always going to be pretty obvious, right? Yet I couldn't just admit to it, could I?

When I hadn't replied after a while, he crossed his arms over his substantial chest and raised his eyebrows. "You're not even going to deny it?"

I inhaled and then exhaled slowly. I had no idea how to navigate this. Nothing in my MBA education or my years of experience running a business had prepared me for handling a professional situation involving my ex. Well, if I could even call him that, so brief our relationship had been. "I'm not sure what you want me to say," I said. At least I was sort of being honest.

A flicker of surprise flashed through his eyes. He studied my face before making a huffing sound and looking away. "I thought you'd continue the ruse, I suppose."

I winced. "There's no ruse." I paused, thinking about how to proceed. "My business intentions have been clear from the start. I haven't been dishonest."

"And me?"

I waited, hoping he'd clarify what he meant. I hoped he didn't mean to ask …

"What were your intentions with me?"

I couldn't stop the sharp intake of breath. "I …" What the hell? How am I supposed to answer that? I swallowed, trying to calm my racing heart.

Think, Mariana, think. Like a businesswoman, not a former lover.

"Terry, you're an important stakeholder, being not only close to the business owner but also a valued employee. A valued contact. It was an obvious choice to try to reconnect with you."

I tried not to shudder. Despite hearing how terrible the

words sounded as I was saying them, I couldn't seem to stop them. And when I saw his face, I died inside. "I … I mean …"

"No, I get it, Mariana. I'm just a dumb shop worker, but I understand. Sorry, I mean, stakeholder." I didn't think his face could show any more loathing if he tried. I had to look away.

Even I—being as emotionally closed off as I was—knew I had to do some damage control. I'd really messed up. "Terry, I didn't mean—"

His posture rigid, he clenched his teeth and then looked at me with deadly calm. "As I said before, it's not going to work. I don't know if you think I'm going to convince Jane to sign over the village to you or what, but it's not happening. Give it up."

My mouth hung open, and I didn't know whether to cry or rage, whether to mourn the loss of his potential help or the loss of … time with him.

Oh, no, no, no. Nope.

I can't be falling for him again. I just can't.

Especially not when he's being so … so horrible. He is, right? Or am I? Oh my god, I just don't know anymore.

Oh, no, he's staring at me. I need to say something. I opened my mouth to reply, but nothing came out.

He shook his head, his lips pressed together. "I mean it. Give up your sad attempt at getting on my good side." He paused and then added, a bit more quietly, "You can just go on living your cushy life, ignoring me like you have since the day we last saw each other all those years ago." His eyes widened slightly and he ran his fingers over his head as though he didn't quite believe what he'd just said, but then he resumed his intense glare. He rose to his feet, as though the conversation were over and he might as well leave.

What?

Wow, he really went there.

I did not expect that. What did he have to gain from dredging up the past, where *he* was in the wrong? I closed my eyes to try to keep my thoughts from straying too far into the past. My voice slightly shaky, I looked up at him and said, "You keep saying that, but we both know that's not what happened."

"Oh, isn't it though? You forgot me immediately, without so much as a 'nice knowing you.'"

I stood then, fury rising within me. Hell no. I was definitely not going to let him get away with this. "I forgot nothing! *You* are the one who didn't respond, who didn't meet me—"

He looked shocked and then even angrier. "Nice one, Mariana. Revisionist history doesn't look good on you."

"W—what are you saying?" I asked, my voice trembling along with my body. "Are you calling me a liar?"

His jaw tense, he shook his head. "Your words, not mine. I know what happened and how you ... you never ..." He stopped, wiping his brow. "Never mind. This is pointless."

I wanted to ask what he was going to say, but I was already so close to tears. Angry, frustrated tears, I think, but either way, I couldn't show him that. After a long pause, I nodded slowly, trying to keep my face neutral. "You—you're right. Pointless."

"It always was, wasn't it?"

I turn around, shielding my face. He couldn't see me right now. My eyes were filling with salty tears, and I knew I couldn't stop them. "Yes," I said, hoping my voice was clear and confident.

Exactly the opposite of how I felt.

A painful silence ensued.

Just go, I wanted to say. I can't cry in front of him. I feared my body might be trembling, despite my best efforts.

I heard a footstep, and I thought for a moment he took a step closer, behind me. I must have imagined it though. Before I could blink, I heard his footsteps and then the door, opening and then closed firmly. Not slammed, but ... final.

I collapsed into the chair, letting out the breath I'd held, the feelings I'd held in, everything I couldn't hold back anymore.

The strange thing was, it wasn't terrible. It was like ... a release. Painful, yet my brain was quiet for once. I somehow knew ... I needed this. Just this once. I could feel, and it would be OK. I would—

Clomp, clomp.

I froze. Someone was walking in the hallway outside. Had he come back?

He can't see me like this. No one can.

Oh my god, oh my god. I have to go lock the door.

But by the time I'd dashed for the door, I didn't hear the footsteps anymore.

I was alone.

I leaned my head against the door for a moment before standing and taking a deep breath in.

I was alone.

I was always alone.

And that was for the best. It always had been.

I wiped another tear as I turned to gather my things from the room.

Chapter 11

Hazel booped me on the nose, and I scowled. "A good dose of holiday decoration is what you need, Mari." She giggled then. "Words I never thought I'd utter to my formerly holiday-hating BFF."

I tried to smile. Failed, utterly.

"Aww, you really don't think you can win him over?" She put a hand on my shoulder and squeezed briefly before taking some more of the red string lights I was unraveling. We'd just started decorating the ballroom for the annual staff holiday party tonight. I normally delegated this to the other leadership, but Hazel convinced me we should help out.

I sighed. "Let's just say it's a lost cause."

She put her hands on her hips, which showed off her sparkly red ugly Christmas sweater dress. "Is he that much of a jerk? Or ... did he do something to you?"

"No, not really," I said, avoiding her eyes. "I just can't get along with him."

Her eyes widened. "The Mariana charm doesn't work on him?"

"Haha, very funny." I rolled my eyes as I held out the last of this string of lights.

She gave me a thoughtful look before taking them. "You think I was joking?"

"I know you were."

She shook her head. "You can be very charming. I've seen you in action. Many times. In some really challenging situations with very difficult people."

I sighed, rolling my shoulders, which were getting a bit sore. "This is a lot different. He hates me. Resents me, for some reason ... which makes no sense, since it should be the other way around. I mean, he's the one—but whatever. Like I said, lost cause."

She paused and then turned to finish hanging up this section of lights.

Ugh, I was oversharing. I needed to change the subject. "You're not wearing that to the party, are you?"

She turned around and grinned. "I should, right? But no, don't worry. I wouldn't dream of breaking the dress code."

I nodded, relieved.

"I mean, unless you changed it," she said while opening up another box of lights.

I gasped. "What?"

"You could change it," she said, looking at me directly for a moment before looking back down at the box she was prying open.

"I ... it's possible, yes. But that would just be ..." I trailed off, unsure what word I was looking for. "Wrong?"

She set the box down for a moment and turned to face me fully. "Why would it be wrong, Mari?"

I opened my mouth to speak and then closed it a few times. "Be—because that's how we do it. Formal. It's—it makes sense. We cater to the wealthy. They like formal. And it's ... professional." My eyes searched hers frantically looking for validation, unsure why I needed it. "And it's always been done that way. It's supposed to be—"

"Mari, Mari," she said, her lips curling in a sympathetic smile. "Take a few breaths."

I obeyed. Once my heart rate settled slightly, I resumed my reasoning. "Holiday parties are traditionally formal, especially when our guests are wealthy and accustomed to luxury. We always have a few guests who drop in every year, so it's not just our staff. We have an image to maintain. We can't have everyone showing up in jeans and flannels."

Hazel looked irritated. "Mari, isn't the party for your staff? Should we be trying to make them comfortable? I wonder if some of them even own formal wear."

"I can say with absolute certainty," came a deep voice from somewhere off to the side, "that many of them don't."

I turned to look at him, shocked. What was he doing *here*? My shock and confusion quickly turned to indignation. "And how would you know?"

"Because I'm friends with many of them. And I know someone who works part-time at the formalwear rental place. Actually, I believe you met Cynthia before too." Cynthia again. What was she to him? I wanted to probe, somehow, but one look at him stopped that line of thought. Though his posture was relaxed, his eyes were cold and cutting. "So, yeah. Your little party costs your staff a lot of money every year, just to attend."

I felt sick to my stomach. Shame washed over me, and I wanted to disappear.

"I'm sorry," I managed to say.

Hazel put her arm around my shoulders. "That was never her intention, Terry. Mariana has a good heart. She values people and takes care of them." She looked at me for a moment as if deciding whether to say more and then turned back to him. "You don't know her very well, do you?"

I saw his jaw muscles flex, and his eyes shifted from her to me. Finally, he just sighed. "It's none of my business."

"Indeed." Hazel raised her eyebrows.

I finally found my voice and lifted my chin, attempting some authority in the place I owned. "So, what are you doing here?"

His eyes darted to the door and back, and he said gruffly, "I got the trees in the truck. Came in to ask where you want them first."

"The trees?" Hazel peered at him and then me, obviously confused.

"I got a call that a big delivery was needed at the castle this morning," he said, ignoring Hazel and looking at me.

My brows furrowed, I nodded slowly. "I did put in an order last night, yeah." I turned to Hazel. "I always feel bad for the smaller, barer trees that no one wants, so I asked them for a dozen to be sent here this morning." When her eyes widened, I added, "For tonight's party."

My best friend's jaw hung open. "You feel bad … for the *trees*?" Before I could reply, she added, "Wait, do we have to decorate all of these before tonight, Mari?"

I smiled. "Don't worry, I have a plan. We have a massive amount of old garland in storage that we never use, and it won't take long. Even Jeff said he'd help."

"Jeff?" She raised her eyebrows in disbelief. "I don't know what's more shocking. That you—"

"Anyway," I interrupted, turning back to Terry. "Um, I guess, thank you for delivering them. Are you … so you work at the tree farm too?"

He stared at me for a moment, and I couldn't read his expression. "I work there. It's mine."

My eyes went wide, and my mouth curled into a reluctant smile. "Seriously? You sell Christmas trees?"

His face hardened then, his eyes steel as he muttered, "I know, it's no shining resort on a hill."

My face fell. "That's not—I didn't mean it like that. I thought … I think it's cool."

He wasn't looking at me though.

Hazel stepped closer to me again. "Not that you deserve it, but I think she's kinda paying you a compliment. She loves Christmas."

His dark eyes changed then, looking more vulnerable as they shifted from Hazel to me. He seemed to want to speak, or maybe ask a question. Finally, he said, "Well, I ought to go get those trees."

"Uh, do you need help?" I asked, my voice obviously reluctant.

He let out a small laugh. "Not really. They're small trees,

like you asked for."

I nodded as he turned around, heading out the door. I might've watched his fine form a little too long because Hazel was eyeing me suspiciously when I finally turned back to her.

"A lost cause, eh?"

"I mean, obviously, right? You saw how badly that went," I said, shaking my head. "Hopeless."

Her lips twisted into a half smile. "Right…" Something about the way she held out the single syllable didn't sit right with me. "Well, listen, I have to go call my agent. You'll be OK here for a bit, right? Shouldn't be too long, and then Jeff and the others will be here at noon, right?"

"Janine said Jeff might be running a little late, but her managers would all be there," I explained. "I'm hoping we'll have most of it done so they can go early." But I cringed, thinking about what many of my staff would be doing when they got home. Worrying about whether their clothes would make the grade, whether they could afford their rent because they had to rent a suit or buy a fancy dress they'd never wear anywhere else.

"Don't do that," she said, watching me carefully. "I see what you're doing. You didn't realize until today. Know better, do better, right? You can change the dress code for next year."

I looked at her, feeling some fear inexplicably, even though it was the right thing to do. I nodded, swallowing down the fear.

"You care about your people, Mari, I know you do," Hazel said. "That's why we got here at 6 am today to decorate. And your managers are helping us. Guess what most fancy resort owners would do? They wouldn't lift a finger. They'd have their lowest-paid staff do it. And those lowest-paid staff? They'd probably be working at the party, not attending it as guests."

I bit my lip, nodding a little. That was one change I'd made when I took over ownership—I'd made sure we hired caterers and outside staff to work the party. No resort staff had to actually serve at the party. If someone did, in an emergency, they were paid triple. I hadn't ever considered this to be generosity but more of a result of my own experiences working here in the past as part of the lowest-tiered staff. "I guess so."

"I know so." Hazel looked at me a bit sadly. I could read her, just as she read me. She was thinking, *Poor Mari is a wonderful person and doesn't realize it.*

But sometimes she was wrong.

With these thoughts, I waved to her and then headed toward the supply closet. Before I reached it though, Terry walked in, carrying the first tree. He looked around and, when he saw me, approached quickly.

"You never answered earlier. Where do you want these?" His voice was monotone. I couldn't see his eyes, hidden behind the evergreen.

I attempted a polite smile. "You're right, I didn't. Sorry. I was thinking they could line those three walls at roughly equal intervals. So, that first one could go—" I stopped then, as he'd turned around and started walking toward the wall behind us, where he promptly put the tree down.

I just stared as he started quickly setting it up in the holder. Rushing over, I called out, "Oh, I can help. Or …" My voice died. "Looks like you got it," I added weakly.

He stood quickly. "Yep." Just like that, he turned and marched away.

I stood, mouth agape.

Well, OK then.

That's how this was going to work.

Furrowing my eyebrows, I tapped my foot as I waited for him to return with another one and moved to the part of the wall where I wanted the next one. The least I could do was tell him where to put it. I was good at directing people, at least.

When he returned, I noticed a slight sheen of sweat on his temple, and he still had his knit hat on. I shook my head, reminding myself to pay attention. "Oh, uh, no, I want that one over here."

He stilled. He'd just squatted to begin putting the trunk in the holder. His eyes swung over to me. "What?"

I cleared my throat. Wasn't I clear? "I said I want that tree over here. About where I'm standing." I paused, but he didn't move. "Can you move it over here?"

His eyes bore into mine. Finally, he stood slowly, and his jaw ticked in visible frustration. "Yes, ma'am."

Ugh. I couldn't make him hate me more if I tried.

I moved away slightly when he came closer.

"Right here?" he asked. "Or here?" He pointed a few inches to the left. "Or maybe over there?"

I bit my tongue slightly. "Here is good. Great, actually." I jumped back, as he was radiating tension and resentment. "Uh, I ... sorry this is such an inconvenience for you."

He didn't say a word as he quickly got the tree set up. But when he stood up, he looked me dead in the eye and said, "Eh, don't worry about it. It's not every day I get to visit the castle." His lips twitched just slightly, and then he walked off.

My wide eyes stayed on him as he walked away. He'd sounded ... almost friendly. Or joking. Maybe there was still a chance I could get him to not hate me?

But did it even matter? Even if I made a little progress, he was determined not to help me with Jane.

Still, I had to try, right? I didn't want him to hate me, did I?

Wait, did I?

I didn't even know anymore.

One thing was for certain. I was starting to think, maybe ... just maybe ... I didn't hate him anymore.

And it scared the hell out of me.

But I found myself meeting him at the door next time, walking him over to the place where the next tree was to be placed. We didn't need to speak much but fell into a comfortable silence as I helped with the placement and setup of the next few trees.

The tension seemed to dissipate, or at least the anger. Maybe there was a different kind of tension. But that was probably just me, my awkwardness. Whatever happened to the cool Mariana who was in control, I had no idea. I missed her. But ... well, I couldn't do anything about it.

So I followed him. I waited at the door when he went outside. When he brought the eighth tree in, he was carrying it on one shoulder, and I could see his face as I stood waiting. It was taller than the others but much thinner in its branches.

And he gave me a small smile. He probably thought I was staring at him, not the tree.

Whatever. I *had* been staring at the tree.

But now … That smile. It was so quick, I could've missed it. But it was everything.

I felt like a bit of Mariana Northam died, and the worst part was, I couldn't even bring myself to care that much.

*****

Sneaking glances at Terry as we walked to the other side of the ballroom, I asked, "Could I set this one up?"

His eyebrows rose. "Hmm."

I scoffed. "What, you don't think I can?" I held up a bicep. "I work out, you know."

His lips tugged up at the corners as his eyes darted down to my silly display of strength and then back up to my face. "I'm sure you do. But you're also a little clumsy. At least in my presence."

"Oh, you—" I sputtered, "it's not *you*. And I'm not clumsy. It's probably an inner ear thing that controls balance, you know. I was planning to call my doctor, actually—"

He chuckled. "Relax, Mariana. I was just playing with you. You can do the tree if you want."

My face relaxed, even as I'm sure it was probably a few shades of pink. He was teasing me. He couldn't hate me if he was teasing, right? Another possible sign that maybe, just maybe, all was not lost. "Really?" I said hopefully.

He shrugged. "It's your tree."

When we got to the wall where I wanted this tree placed, I worked slowly on the base. I'd helped my dad with this when I was little, but it had been so long. I didn't want to mess it up.

I had to unscrew the different sides a few times when it seemed tilted, and Terry took hold of the tree when it seemed that it might tip over.

"Thanks," I mumbled.

Maybe I should make small talk. This was not the most uncomfortable silence ever, but it was not exactly pleasant either.

"So, a tree farm, eh? Is this just … an extra income thing or a particular interest of yours?"

He didn't answer for a long time. Finally, I looked up at him, curious at whether he'd even heard me.

"Both, I guess."

I thought about how to respond to this. "Really? You're interested in Christmas trees? Or farming? Or retail or … what part of it is your interest?"

I heard him take a few breaths before he responded. "All of the above, I guess." I thought he wasn't going to say anymore, but after a very long pause, he added, "I got a botany degree a couple years ago. And I like this area, so … finding some unconventional ways to put it to use, I guess."

"Wow, that's … really wonderful," I said. A botanist? What on earth? I never would've guessed. Of all the things. "It's great to have an occupation that is rewarding in more than just money."

"Is that how owning an elite resort is for you? Or is it just about the money?" His voice had an unmistakable note of derision in it.

I felt my hackles go up again as I turned to him. "Why would you just assume that? Is it that hard to imagine that I might enjoy what I do?"

I pushed up with my feet then, trying to stand, but I lost my footing while trying to hold onto the tree. I started taking the tree with me as I went crashing back to the floor, my shoulder blades hitting the wall. Dammit, that hurt.

Just before the tree trunk crashed into my face though, a large hand wrapped around it, and Terry's solid form fell against my side.

"Oof!" I think I said, or maybe it was him. He carefully set the tree further aside so it leaned against the wall before starting to back away from me, and in the meantime, I couldn't breathe.

It was getting hard to be so close to him. More like impossible. I couldn't do it. I couldn't breathe or think. I couldn't —

"Mariana, are you all right?" He looked concerned. "Your breathing … are you hurt?"

I just looked at him, my lips unable to form words.

His eyebrows drew together as he looked at my hunched form, and he touched my upper arms gently, so gently I thought I would cry. "Mariana, please. Where are you hurt? What can I do?"

I had to speak, or … I didn't know what would happen. I took a few breaths, trying to steady my racing heart, with little success. "M-my shoulder hit the wall."

His eyes darted to my left shoulder and then my right and then back to my face. "Which one? How bad is it?" His face made a pained expression before he added, "Do you think it's dislocated?"

My eyes widened. "Oh, uh, no. They both hurt, but I … I'll be fine. It's not that bad. I'm just … I'm OK."

The reactions on his face changed so many times I lost count, but eventually he settled on frustrated, with a touch of confusion. "So, you're not really hurt? You're just fine?"

I tried to smile. "Right. It just took the wind out of my sails, you know."

He looked at me with some doubt but started to rise to his feet. "All right."

"I'll just ice it later or something. It's no big deal." It would probably be a pain in the butt, actually, as my neck and shoulders tended to be sensitive in the past year, especially when I was stressed, but I'd deal with that later. Now wasn't the time to worry about that. I needed to get distance. Now.

"Do you need a hand?" he asked as I started getting up,

holding onto the wall for support.

I shook my head no. In truth, it would've been helpful to have assistance … from anyone but him. I couldn't handle him touching me again, even for something so innocent as a helping hand up from the floor.

Fresh on my feet, I forced an optimistic smile. "All right, where was I?" Time to finish that damn tree and the others so Terry could go home and leave me alone.

I reached for the tree, but his back was to me and he reached for it too and swung it sideways, pushing me back against the wall a couple of feet.

The shock of the push knocked the wind out of my lungs for a moment, but I didn't fall this time, at least, thanks to a last-minute decision to brace my feet strategically apart.

Terry, seeing that he'd accidentally caused the tree trunk to slam me against the wall, let out a string of curses and slammed the tree on the floor.

I watched in shock as some branches snapped off. The poor little thing. I'd already felt sorry for it, being the runt of the tree farm, most likely. My eyes swung cautiously back up to him, standing close enough that I could see the different shades of brown in his dark eyes, which seemed closer to black than usual.

"Dammit, woman, why are you so accident-prone?" he thundered. His brows furrowed, and anger laced his tone as he braced his hands on the wall.

I breathed. In and out. It was all I could do. I felt the wetness in my eyes and the pounding in my chest. Finally, I licked my parched lips and choked out, "I—I don't know." Why was I such a disaster around him? Maybe I didn't want to know.

He looked into my eyes, and for a moment I thought he seemed closer somehow, though I'm pretty sure he hadn't moved and I hadn't moved. And then he looked past me, at the wall I suppose. His eyes returned to mine, dark and piercing as ever. His voice was quiet and deep. "And why, Mariana … why can't I walk away?"

"Walk away?"

I barely got the words out, when suddenly he leaned in and his lips found mine as his fingers slid into my hair, and I quickly lost all ability to think. No tentative, tender kisses for us—we immediately went for deep, thorough, I-want-to-climb-you kisses. My fingers played with his hair, stroked his stubbly cheeks, and tested the solidness of those muscled arms. I pressed against him, needing to be as close as possible, our tongues tangling in a battle of who could go deeper, who could draw out the most passion from the other. Surely, I would win, but maybe it would be a tie—he was like a man starved as he kissed me like he hadn't kissed in ages.

"From you." He started a trail of kisses and nibbles along my jaw. "Why can't I walk away from you?"

"Oh, I …" I couldn't think. What was he even talking about? I had to get closer. I hitched my leg around his hip, and he groaned but then smiled before taking my lips again, his hand possessively gripping my hip.

But then he moved his hand back to my hair, my leg kicked out, and—

Crash.

He jerked his lips away, untangling our limbs a bit more slowly as we both turned confused faces toward the sound.

The tree.

Lying on the floor.

I must have kicked the tree over.

And…

We had been …

No. *No. We couldn't.*

Oh my god, what had we done?

My eyes were huge as I stared at him with my chest heaving. His hair was disheveled, his shirt collar messed up, and he looked like he had no idea where he was.

Same, Terry, same.

Not thinking clearly, I put my finger on my lips, as if needing to feel the evidence … yep, I'd just been thoroughly kissed.

And he was staring at my mouth. Was he looking at the lipstick that was probably smeared on my chin? Or did he want to …

"Um." I had to say something. But what?

It was enough. It seemed to break the spell, and his expression slowly shuttered as his eyes swept the scene around us and finally landed back on me.

His voice sounded a little hoarse, but his eyes betrayed none of his feelings. "Why'd you change your name?"

I raised my eyebrows slightly, unprepared for that question. I looked down, suddenly embarrassed about this for the first time. I don't even know why—I'd always considered the name change—the identity change—one of the best decisions I'd ever made. "Uh, it's complicated—"

"You're not married."

My eyes flew from the floor to his face, seeing some uncertainty there. "Of course not. No. Never married." Why oh *why* did I volunteer that extra tidbit? Make it really obvious I'd never gotten serious with anyone after him. I sighed. "I just needed a new start."

"Why?"

"The old me was going nowhere in life, if you hadn't noticed." I laughed bitterly. "But you were too privileged back then to notice."

"Was I? You assume a lot about me." A strange glint appeared in his eyes before he looked away.

I didn't know what to say to this. "Well, anyway." How to end this awkward conversation that occurred after that awkward—oh my god, we kissed. Shouldn't we be talking about *that*? Or maybe not. Probably best to sweep it under the rug, just like the past was. My heart was still fluttering as I made a show of looking at my watch. "Actually, some of my helpers will arrive soon, and I have some business to attend to in my office. Do you mind finishing up the tree placement without me?"

He looked at me with eyes that saw far, far too much. Goddammit, since when did I become so transparent? After an awkward pause, he nodded slowly. "Sure thing, boss."

    I gave him a polite smile, which felt ridiculous under the circumstances. I might as well have curtsied. He merely tipped his chin and bent to pick up the tree. As I turned to escape though, he called out, "Might want to fix your lipstick, princess."

    I pivoted with a scowl, but he'd already kneeled down to set up the troublesome tree. Huffing just loud enough for him to hear, I spun around and nearly ran out of the ballroom and back to my suite.

Chapter 12

Wiping my brow, I returned the whiskey to its place of honor on the shelf. I tried to ignore the ache in my heels and lower back. I went to the staff gym often enough and considered myself reasonably in shape, but I wasn't used to working on my feet for hours. It had been too long. I suppose it didn't help that I'd spent the afternoon rage-skating on the frozen lake in the woods behind the resort, followed by an hour of online Christmas shopping hunched over on the floor with my laptop.

"Mari!" called an out-of-breath Hazel as she approached. "I've been looking everywhere for you. Have you …" She looked around, her brow furrowed. "Tell me you haven't been serving drinks all night."

I shook my head slightly as I started pouring her favorite drink. "Where's your date?"

She pulled out a stool and put her elbows on the counter I'd just cleaned. She waved a hand behind her in a vague motion. "Somewhere." When I raised my eyebrows, she sighed. "I gave up. He was flirting with some girl named Cynthia. Seemed sweet, but really young. Not going to waste my time, you know?"

I looked behind Hazel, trying to find the guy I'd seen her with earlier. When I spotted him, he was indeed talking to Cynthia. Or dancing, actually.

My lips started curving into a smile. Wait, why am I happy about this? It doesn't matter if Cynthia is flirting with someone. Why would I care?

Because maybe then she's not flirting with Terry.

Or maybe she's just a flirt. It doesn't mean anything one way or another. There *could* still be something between her and Terry *even if* she flirts with other guys.

I frowned deeply. *Ugh, shut up, insecure Mari.* It matters not at all. Terry isn't anything to me anymore. He and Cynthia can go have babies for all I care. But I don't. Care, that is.

But just the thought of him having babies with her—or anyone … I felt my breath quicken, and I wiped the counter down again briskly.

When I looked up at Hazel, she was giving me a strange look but then took a sip of her drink. "*So.*" She paused then, as though waiting for me to continue.

I wasn't sure what she wanted me to say, but I cleared my throat and gave it my best shot. "Sorry to hear your date was a disappointment, Haz—"

"Pshh." She waved her hands, cutting me off. "I don't care about him. I want to know why you've been tending bar all night."

I opened my mouth to reply but then closed it. I pretended to clean a shot glass nearby that was already clean. "The one we hired wasn't working out. I had to send her home. And … well, I didn't want to make my own staff work during the party."

She raised an eyebrow. She didn't believe me, and with good reason, I suppose. "Right." She finished off her drink with a long swig. "Now," she said, leaning forward, "tell me the real reason."

I forced myself to maintain eye contact. "I don't mind, you know. I used to tend bar many years ago, and I was pretty good at it. One of my many odd jobs from the past." She kept looking at me with a challenge in her eyes. "And I did spend over an hour mingling at the beginning of the night, so don't worry—I wasn't neglecting my host duties."

She shook her head, crinkling her eyes. "I wasn't *worried* about—Mari, come on." She leaned forward, making intense eye contact. "You know what I'm asking."

What was she talking about? Whatever it was, I felt the urge to laugh nervously, but I stifled it.

"Uh, I don't think I do." I heard my voice shake a little as I looked desperately to the side to see if anyone else was approaching the bar. There was one woman, but the sole bartender at the other end was greeting her.

Hazel stared at me for a moment, narrowing her eyes. Finally, she abruptly sat back in her seat, and her eyes flashed in annoyance.

"Hazel? What's—"

She looked away for a moment and then turned accusing eyes at me once again. "I saw you!"

I swallowed. "You saw ... what do you mean?"

"Mari, just cut the crap. For once in your life." She shook her head. I couldn't remember the last time I'd seen her this angry, at least not at me. "I saw you and Terry."

At my sharp intake of breath, she laughed bitterly. "Yeah, that. Were you going to tell me?"

I had to stop wiping the counter and gripped the edge of it instead. Shock turned to dismay and then embarrassment and then regret. "Hazel, I ..." I stopped, not knowing what to say. "I'm sorry."

She looked away for a long moment, shaking her head at first.

"Sorry, it's just ... I guess I didn't know what to think. How to process it. I think I would've told you." I bit my lip, realizing too late that wasn't the right thing to say.

"You *think*? But you're not sure? Maybe you would've kept that from your best friend, maybe not?" When our eyes met again, this time she just looked disappointed.

"I didn't mean that. I would've told you." I looked at her, and she looked unconvinced. "Or you would've dragged it out of me eventually. Because you have that superpower." I tried to give her a weak smile.

She didn't speak for a while, and she definitely didn't smile. "You're right, I would've. But I shouldn't have to, dammit.

Don't you just … want to tell me things? Your best friend?"

Looking at her face, a picture of hurt, I swallowed and nodded. "It's hard for me though." I sighed. And I'm not all that convinced that talking to anyone about feelings, or having anything to do with them, is even a good idea … but I knew it was the wrong time to say that. "But yes, and I'm sorry. Truly."

After a long moment, she squeezed my hand. "So, Mari, what are we going to do about him?"

My eyes widened. She didn't mean … oh wait, she means the business deal. My shoulders sagged in relief. "Well, the plan to make him an ally was doomed anyway, so I'll probably just need to go straight to Jane and figure out what is really going through her mind. We don't really know why she won't sell, so I think—"

"Stop, Mari. I wasn't talking about the business thing. I mean we can talk about that, but what about you and your long-lost love?"

I felt my lips twist in amusement. "My what? This isn't a Hallmark movie."

"But it could be," she said with a grin as her Santa hat started to fall off her head.

I saved it before it could land on the counter. "There's no long-lost anything, and certainly not … love." The word was hard to say. It felt bittersweet, and I felt a pang in my chest. Ugh, heartburn again probably.

Hazel gave me the sympathetic look she'd given me many times when she thought I was missing out on something, usually because I liked being rational, staying in the present, and working hard. I didn't let it bother me usually. But tonight, I found myself feeling that pang again. I needed to find the antacids. I was about to ask if she had any in her red and green purse when she spoke, "I saw that kiss. I don't think you can just sweep it under the rug like you usually do." She paused, furrowing her eyebrows upon seeing my resolved expression. "But you're going to try, aren't you?"

I bit my lip and then nodded with a sheepish smile. "Hey, I

can probably get Ted down there to cover the bar now that it's so late. Want to go raid the dessert table and put our feet up?"

My friend's eyes lit up. "I thought you'd never ask."

Chapter 13

I'd just removed my boots when I felt my phone buzz in my pocket.

Now what? I sighed. I'd just finished helping calm a very confused older woman who was found making snow angels outside while singing something unrecognizable but vaguely resembling a Christmas tune. Of course, I'd had the night off, but the staff informed me that this woman also happened to be the wife of a high-ranking senator, so we needed to treat this one with kid gloves. Sigh. Once we had her safely back in her room, I'd reminded the night manager in no uncertain terms that I was off-duty tonight.

So it was with great annoyance that I pulled my phone out, expecting I was needed yet again. But the corner of my lips turned upward when I saw the sender of the text.

Hazel: Merry Christmas Eve!

Hazel: Or should I say Mari Christmas? Hahaha I'm so funny

Me: You missed your calling as a comedian.

Hazel: I know! Listen, I wanted to call but Mom and I are on this Christmas Eve cruise on the Seine, and it's SO loud. There's nowhere quiet. How are you?

As always, Hazel had invited me to her family holiday, and as always, I'd declined. I didn't have a good reason. Who wouldn't want to spend Christmas in Paris? Hazel's mom was Jewish but always went all out for Christmas. I'd never understood, but her entire family was a big, strange, wonderful thing of beauty that I'd long ago learned not to question.

Well, I did have a reason for declining. I liked staying here, by myself. It wasn't a good reason, I supposed. But I wanted—no, I needed—to keep Dad's memory alive. Gallivanting across the globe and attending a glitzy party wasn't Dad's style at all, and even though I'd changed a lot since I was a kid, I needed to feel close to him on Christmas, at least.

I texted her back "I'm good," as one does when trying to not burden someone else with their woes. I set the phone down on the kitchen island as I rifled around in the fridge.

My face clouded over when I saw how empty it was. Dammit, I was going to head to the store yesterday and completely forgot. It had been a fairly busy week. Well, technically not that busy, but I'd kept myself busy. With Hazel gone and that annoying holiday loneliness setting in, I knew that keeping myself busy would be key. I'd planned a rigid routine of working, exercising, redecorating my dining room, and plotting some new approaches to try with Jane after the holiday. But with yesterday's personnel crisis—and that's putting it mildly, since it ended with two valets in the hospital—I'd totally forgotten to restock the fridge. And the pantry.

Ugh.

Would any stores even be open this late on Christmas Eve?

I picked up my phone to look up some places.

Hazel: You're good? What are you doing tonight?

Hazel: Revealing as always, I see. ;) Well, you're lucky I'm having a blast here so I'll let it go. I'll text you later, Mari.

Hazel: Lots of love, talk tomorrow

Me: Sorry, just stepped away for a bit. I'll be OK. Have a great night!!

I'm not normally an exclamation point sort of woman—much less double exclamation points—but I wanted Hazel to have fun and not worry about me. She did spend too much time worrying about me, didn't she? Ugh. So unnecessary, especially since I was always fine. Just fine.

After finding the address of the one store in town still open, I hurried to get my winter gear back on. I had to bundle up, and the place was closing in an hour.

At the store, I was scanning the label outside of the aisle when something caught my attention from the side. I swung my eyes over and nearly gasped aloud. How is it possible we've lived in the same area for years and never encountered each other, yet all the sudden I run into him *everywhere*?

Before I could think about how stupid my action would be, I ducked into a different aisle and pulled my thick brown hat down over my forehead and eyebrows.

And I left my cart at the end of the other aisle. Heart pounding, I tried to think fast. Would it be better to just run? Did I have a clear path to the exit from here? This was row 7.

I shook my head and took a deep breath.

Get a grip.

This is insanity.

With that, I slowly walked back around to where I'd left the shopping cart, trying to peer in all directions at once.

When my hands landed on the cart, I let out a sigh of relief.

No sign of Terry now.

Had I even seen him before, or was I now imagining him in odd places? I *did* find myself thinking about him a ridiculous amount this week. Not exactly conjuring his actual appearance, but it had been a long day, a long week, perhaps I'd hallucinated it. Wishful thinking. How stupid, and how unlike me.

I took another slow, steady breath and looked at the exit door.

Maybe I should just leave.

Screw this.

Sure, having food is nice, but was it worth running into him?

I bit my lip and then nearly laughed at my own indecision. How ridiculous. I proceeded to walk down aisle 6 and tried to focus on my shopping list.

By aisle 13, I'd forgotten about him as I carefully examined the labels of 14 different kinds of caramel ice cream. They all looked so good, but I didn't have a huge freezer (by design, thanks to a little ice cream addiction), so I was limiting myself to one. Maybe two.

OK, I'd probably get three or four.

No more than five.

I was juggling six little tubs of different varieties of caramel ice cream in my arms and walking back to my cart when my heart lodged in my throat.

Those eyes, that face, that man … not just my imagination, no. He was striding down the aisle with a small basket. His eyes went straight to the ice cream, and several little tubs promptly rolled out of my arms.

He reached me just as they started rolling on the floor in different directions, and of course, he had to help pick them up.

"Hosting an ice cream party tonight, Mariana?" His voice was tinged with amusement.

I didn't look up, merely grabbed the last two tubs from the floor and rose, bringing them to my shopping cart.

He followed me over and dropped in the tubs he'd picked up.

Finally, I looked him in the eye, raising my chin. "Maybe I am."

He looked at a few of the labels. "Looks like all your guests have very specific taste."

"Yeah, it's pretty exclusive."

His lips curled into an almost-smile. "Maybe I'll host my own party for the chocolate and strawberry ice cream fans."

"You do that. I can't be friends with those people." I fought the urge to smile.

Were we actually joking with each other? Making friendly conversation?

I needed to nip this in the bud. I can't do casual conversations with him. I just can't be around him, period.

I wiped my expression of any humor and offered a polite nod. "Well, if you'll excuse me, I need to go."

Without looking back, I turned to push my cart in the opposite direction where he was standing.

But when I was only a few steps away, I thought I heard him call out, "OK, have a good Christmas."

My feet stopped, and I turned slowly, reluctantly. He was still standing there, looking at me with an unreadable expression. "What?"

"I said, Merry Christmas," he said as he leaned against one of the coolers.

"I …" I couldn't speak, couldn't move.

I was brought back to that Christmas Eve, all those years ago.

When we were supposed to meet again.

When he didn't show.

When I wanted to kick myself for showing up, since he'd never bothered to keep in touch.

When I thought I'd learned my lesson.

Yet here I was, drawn to him, again.

His dark brows furrowed as he intently watched the emotions pass over my face. "Mariana?" My name rolled off his lips so slowly, and he took a couple of tentative steps toward me, but we were still several paces apart.

I licked my parched lips and briefly squeezed my eyes shut. "Sorry, I am, yes, good Christmas to you too. I mean, Merry Christmas."

He took another step toward me, this time more deliberately. "Are you all right? You look …"

"I'm fine," I said quickly, my breath coming fast.

What a liar I was. And the look on his face told me that he knew it, too.

He eyed me for a very long moment, and my eyes darted from him to the floor and back to him. "What are your plans?"

"My plans? For ... what?" Lost in his eyes, I was finding it hard to think. Not hard—impossible. What was he talking about anyway?

"Your plans for the Christmas holiday?" He took a longer breath. "For tonight?"

I'm sure the shade of pink on my flushed face darkened, and I averted my eyes.

Oh, that's what he's asking. Um ...

"Oh, just the usual, nothing very fancy. How about you?" I started to fidget with the scarf hanging from my neck.

He ignored my question. "What's the usual?"

If my heart were racing before, it was on track to win the race now. "Oh, you know, lots of eating, Christmas tunes, trees, naps. Maybe a festive movie. Just like anyone else." I forced my lips into what I hoped looked like a convincing smile.

He nodded slightly. "Do you celebrate with family? Or friends? I'm thinking you must celebrate tomorrow if tonight is grocery night."

For some reason, even though he didn't matter—he didn't!—I didn't want him to know that I celebrated alone, or not at all. That I had for many years. That I hated it, even though I usually enjoyed my own company. That I missed having a family Christmas, that I wished Hazel wouldn't always travel for the holiday but I always wanted the best for her.

"Why the 20 questions, Terry?" I asked, putting my hands on my hips.

A flash of hurt passed over his face, and I instantly regretted the abrupt question. His shoulders slunk. "Sorry, I was just thinking maybe—you know, never mind. Sorry to bother you."

The despair on his face tugged at my heart, and I had a feeling he was about to walk away now. Suddenly I had to make things right. Even though I was so close to getting rid of him now, like I'd wanted.

"Wait, what were you thinking?" When he didn't reply right away and just shook his head, I added, "Sorry if I was rude. I just … my holiday plans aren't very exciting. That is, I don't have any." I was going to regret saying that, probably, but so be it. I couldn't handle the hurt in his eyes, especially if I'm the one who put it there. But I could handle a little humiliation if I could make him less sad.

I heard myself think, and I had to wonder: Who was this Mariana? I bit my lip.

His eyes rose to meet mine, and we just stayed that way for a long time.

Finally, he took another tentative step toward me. "I'm not busy tonight either. And it just so happens …" His mouth curved into a slow grin. "I like caramel ice cream too. With strawberry."

My eyes widened. "What? No, you can't mix caramel with fruit! You're ruining the caramel flavor. Well, I guess the exception is apples. Who doesn't love a caramel apple, am I right?" I stopped then, remembering the other part of what he'd said.

Was he suggesting …

No, he couldn't be.

My brows scrunched together, I looked at him for answers, unwilling to guess at his meaning and risk looking like a fool.

"Come to my place. And bring your ice cream."

He *was* suggesting it.

My eyes searched his face, looking for the punchline, but he just looked at me steadily. "Well, I don't think … I mean, that's kind—"

"Nothing kind about it. I'm selfish." He smirked.

"Terry—" I didn't know how to say this, but I had to tell him no. I had to. Didn't I?

"Come over, and I'll prove you wrong."

I inhaled sharply. "Prove … what exactly?" Were my feelings really that obvious?

Wait, I don't have feelings for him. Got to remember that.

He crossed his arms over his wide chest and smiled broadly. "That caramel and strawberry ice cream is the best."

"That is *not* possible. You can't prove something that's …

that's false." I crossed my arms too. "I should get home—"

"I can prove it, and I will. Come, Mariana." He stood a little closer now, and I could see the fire in his beautiful eyes. "Please?"

Oh, no.

Oh, no, no, no, no.

The man said *please*.

I'm a lost cause.

Chapter 14

"It's really quite beautiful, isn't it? Fresh snow on Christmas Eve, some colorful Christmas lights ..." He looked over at me, and I saw his teeth glimmering white as he smiled at me.

"And an actual Christmas tree farm," I finished for him. Terry, as it turns out, lives on the tree farm. Literally. So I guess it makes sense that he sells and delivers them, though he said he actually has a couple employees. He's an entrepreneur, apparently. I'm a little intrigued, though I don't want to be.

He told me all this as we pulled into his long driveway. He convinced me to ride in his truck since he has four-wheel drive and it was snowing pretty heavily by that point.

"Very beautiful," I agreed.

And it was. But inside, I was a mess.

A goddamn mess.

What was I thinking going to his *house*? At *night*? And on this *holiday* night, of all nights?

There were only two ways this night could go, really. We were either going to sleep together or get into an epic argument about the past. Or both.

I wasn't ready for either one.

No, correcting that: I didn't *want* either one.

But here I was.

"Shhh." He gazed at me, having just turned off the car, now in his garage.

Confused, I raise my eyebrows. "I didn't say anything, did

I?" I unbuckled my seat belt. "In fact, it's pretty dead quiet out here."

He looked at me with a gentle smile, one I hadn't seen from the grown-up Terry, well, ever. "I'm shushing the inner Mariana. The one who's overthinking, who's probably trying to come up with excuses to call a cab."

I opened my mouth but then closed it, realizing I couldn't dispute his claim. I sighed. "What is it with you and Hazel thinking you can just guess what I'm thinking at all times?"

He chuckled. "I'm nowhere near Hazel's level. I don't know what you're thinking most of the time. But sometimes … well, sometimes I can tell. You show it, how you're feeling. And I remember."

I felt my breathing coming a bit faster after he said "I remember" but just rolled my eyes, trying to dismiss him. "Think what you want," I grumbled.

"Oh, I plan on it," he said, and I didn't look at him, but I could hear the laughter in his voice. Instead, I focused on getting out of the car.

"We'll probably have to put the ice cream in the freezer for a while, as it's probably soupy by this point," I pointed out as we got the groceries out of the car. "Unless … please tell me you're not one of those people who like soupy ice cream. I'll go home right this instant."

Terry's body shook with laughter as he set down a bag to open the door. "Ah, there's the old Mariana. Fun, feisty … love it. No, I'm not a soupy ice cream fan."

"Oh good," I said, giving him a side eye and trying not to smile. "I was afraid you'd be one of those people who warms it up in the microwave."

He raised his eyebrows. "What? Some people actually do that?" He laughed then as he held the door open for me. I walked through the door and then turned to him to respond. Before he shut the door though, he added, "I like it hard. Real hard."

My cheeks were on fire then, but I tried to shrug it off. "Classy, a sex joke about ice cream."

"Who said anything about a sex joke?" he asked, his voice faux innocent. "Are you thinking about sex, Mariana?" His eyes widened comically.

I shook my head, unable to fight a smile. "You're teasing me, I know. Ha-ha, it's so fun to make the buttoned-up Mariana squirm."

He shrugged, looking into my eyes. "Well, it is."

When I finally dragged my eyes away from his, I scanned the room. We'd entered from the garage into the kitchen. It was kind of an old-fashioned kitchen but relatively tidy. I brought some bags over to the fridge and freezer to begin putting things away.

"I'll give you the grand tour once we get this stuff unloaded," he said. "Let me just go check to make sure the house is in decent shape before I show it off."

He ran off then, and I let out a long exhalation.

Taking a break from freezer loading, I just leaned back against the counter and closed my eyes.

I could do this.

But …

I didn't know what I was doing here.

I didn't know what *he* thought we were doing.

We never really talked about what happened, the kiss a week ago …

But we don't like each other, and we're both resentful. That hasn't changed, has it? It couldn't have changed … the past can't be changed.

Could I do this?

I jumped when he suddenly returned, more quickly than I'd thought. "That was quick."

"Just had to hide one embarrassing thing," he said with a mysterious smile.

Who was this man who kept smiling at me?

He needed to stop it.

It was one thing if I had to spend time with him, but he couldn't keep smiling at me like that. I wouldn't survive it …

"Maybe I'll make you tell me. Got some eggnog? Spiked?"

Wait, what? Drinking was a terrible, terrible idea. Why the hell had I just said that? I clamped my hand over my mouth. "Uh, just kidding. I ... have to drive home, of course."

A wistful smile quickly flashed over his face, and he ran his hands through his dark hair. "No eggnog. No booze at all actually. I don't drink much anymore."

I peered at his face, which was suddenly serious. "Oh, OK, sorry, I didn't mean—"

"No worries. I don't mind if people drink around me. I have a little occasionally. I just don't keep it in the house." He paused then, leaning back against the counter next to me. "My parents ... well, you know they died in an accident, right? Alcohol was involved. They were drinking, and so was the other driver. And Mom had a problem with—" He stopped then, dragging his hand over his jaw. "I don't know why I'm telling you all this. Sorry about the Debbie downer."

My voice was gentle when I responded, "It's OK. I'd like to hear more sometime if you want to talk about it. And no apologies needed, Terry. At least not about *that*."

His head swiveled in my direction, and he raised an eyebrow. "Right, because I've got so many other things to apologize for."

I nodded, my eyebrows raised as if to say, "Of course you do."

He looked at me silently for a long, long moment. Finally, he announced, "Well, let's start the taste test!"

"What?" I frowned. "Surely it's not cold enough yet." I refused to say *hard*.

"No, your new ones won't be. But I have a strawberry caramel swirl already in the freezer. You can try that one." He met my eyes with a look of challenge.

I wrinkled my nose. "You're lucky I don't back down from a challenge. That sounds gross, but sure, bring it on. Hopefully the pure caramel will be ready to eat soon. Since I'll need a palate cleanser."

He smiled again, shaking his head as he dipped down to retrieve the ice cream from behind the ones I'd put in the freezer. "You're going to be eating those words."

"I'll be eating something," I mumbled. Watching as he retrieved some spoons and napkins, I tried not to think about what the hell I was doing here.

I took the spoon from his outstretched hand, careful to avoid touching his hand. "Well, let's get this over with."

"Prepare to have your taste buds ruined for all other ice creams," he said, opening the cover and then handing it to me. "Ladies first."

I took a small, careful bite and closed my eyes, careful to keep any expression off my face as I took in the odd flavor combination. When I opened my eyes, his were focused intently on my mouth.

Was he … no, he's looking at my mouth because I'm eating. He's looking for a reaction to what I'm tasting. With my mouth.

I took another bite, and his eyes didn't leave my face. I didn't miss the tiny intake of breath from him when I licked my lips after swallowing the ice cream.

"All right," I said. He blinked a few times and made eye contact again. "This flavor is OK."

He gasped. "Just *OK*?"

I smirked. "I like it, but I don't love it." I took another bite. "It'll do until the real deliciousness is ready for consumption."

"You're hopeless," he said, shaking his head. "Give me that." But he didn't take the bucket, he just stuck his spoon in the container to take some while I still held it. "It's my favorite. It's the perfect blend of—oh …" His voice trailed off as his hand suddenly rose to touch my chin.

It was just a small brush of his thumb, but I had to fight the urge to jump back. I didn't want him to think I was scared of him. Or scared of … this.

"You had a bit of ice cream there," he explained.

I couldn't look away but just nodded.

He shifted on his feet and looked at something behind me.

"Hey so, um, I didn't get dinner earlier. I was thinking I'd just pop a pizza in the oven. Do you want some or—"

"Yes," I said automatically. Pizza was everything. And I was desperate for a neutral topic. "Please."

"OK, let me go down to the basement freezer real quick," he said, pointing vaguely behind me. "Want to watch a movie?"

It sounded risky, honestly. A movie could be a perfectly platonic thing. Were we friends now? I had no idea. I thought we hated each other. But anyway, platonic. Or *not*. I remembered more than one occasion when we'd watched a movie in his room at the resort when his parents were off dining with some of their fancy friends. We hadn't spent much time watching the movie.

Then again, what else were we going to do? Sit and talk? Argue? Make out? All of those would be far worse. OK, movie it is. I can keep boundaries. We're not dating, like before. It'll be fine, right? It'll be—

"Hey, it's OK. We don't have to," he said gently. My eyes shifted from the vague area of the wall I'd been staring at back to his face. "Doesn't have to be a movie. We could—"

"No, fine," I croaked. "It's fine. Movie, yes."

The corners of his mouth rose just slightly, and he nodded. "OK then. I'll go get that pizza. The TV's in the living room, down that hall. Go pick a movie?"

I nodded, and we stared at each other for another awkward moment before my feet finally started moving toward the hallway.

Approximately two hours later, he flipped off the TV. I turned to him from my end of the couch, which was thankfully quite large, with plenty of space between us. I stretched out my legs a bit. "That was a cute movie."

"I still can't believe you'd never seen *Elf*." He shook his head.

I chuckled. "I know, and you're not the first person to tell me that."

He looked at me from across the couch. "But I'm the first to watch it with you."

Ugh, why was my face heating up? We were just talking about a movie, that's all. At least the lighting was dim. It must be the fireplace.

I made a show of looking at my watch. "Oh, it's later than I realized. Uh, I should probably head home now."

His expression was stoic when he answered, "Well, I don't have a sleigh."

I felt a smile tugging at my lips as I forced myself to rise from the comfortable couch cushions. "I think we'll manage. You don't have to drive me home, just take me back to my car."

I walked over to the wide windows and pulled the curtain back to look outside.

It was the kind of snow that glitters, like something out of a painting. But it was real, here, at—

"Like hell we are," he growled, suddenly so close.

I jumped sideways. He was suddenly right behind me. I swallowed with some effort and then moistened my lips. "It's beautiful out there."

He gazed out the window for a moment, and then I saw his jaw clench as he turned back to me. "It looks like nearly two feet have fallen since we got here. You know the plows won't be out yet."

I opened my mouth, trying to think of a response. I mean, I had to go. What choice did I have? "Terry, it's not the first time I've driven in snow. I'm a Minnesota girl. I'll be fine, if you can just—"

"No." He crossed his arms over his chest, the firm set of his jaw making me doubt myself. "The roads are probably horrible. I won't have you getting into an accident and, I don't know, suing me. Isn't that what people like you do?"

I reared back at the accusation. "You—you think I would ..." I told myself to take measured breaths. He was just angry, for some reason, and lashing out. Why? I didn't know. "I don't know what you mean by 'people like me,' but no, I wouldn't." He just stood there with his arms crossed, an immovable wall. "I have to go, I don't have any other choice—"

"You're staying." He didn't break eye contact.

My eyes widened. "You don't mean … I can't stay *here*. I mean, I could for a little while, but not for long—"

"You're staying." His voice carried a tone of finality.

I was silent for a while, contemplating my choices. Well, they were grim. Basically, I could either stay here or attempt to walk from here to my car, but I didn't really know where I was, and walking in heavy snowfall didn't sound like a great idea.

"It's not your decision to make." I glared at him. "I could … call a cab."

He raised an eyebrow. "And put some innocent driver's life at risk because you couldn't just tough it out until the storm's over and the plows have cleared it out?"

I spun around, needing to have some distance. As I paced, I said, "Fine. Bad idea. I'll stay for a bit," I snapped. "Happy?"

"I'm no happier than you are, Princess," he said with a scowl.

"Then why … why not just take me home?"

"I told you, the roads—"

"I know, but … never mind." I sighed, slowing my steps and turning to face him a few feet away. "I'll stay out of your way. Or maybe the roads will be cleared soon. I'll go look up the weather and road conditions on my phone."

I went to sit on the couch and pulled out my phone.

And it didn't look good. I put my phone down with a long exhale. "Heavy snow predicted through morning." I looked up at him. "Do you have a spare room? If not, the couch is fine. I mean it, I'll stay out of your way."

He turned around to look out the window for a long moment, and the silence was painful.

I can't believe I got myself into this mess. I shouldn't even be here in the first place.

"I'm sorry. I shouldn't even be here. I promise not to be a bother if—"

"Shhh," he said, loud enough for me to hear even though he hadn't turned around to look at me.

"I mean, why am I even here? We don't even like each other. And on Christmas Eve of all days," I said bitterly, remembering the one where he didn't show up—where I was a goddamn fool for ever thinking he would.

He finally turned around and strode over to the couch. "Shhh," he said again while holding out a hand to me. I stared at it, unsure what to make of this gesture. "Take my hand."

I didn't want to. I mean, I did want to. But it was the last thing I should do.

So, of course I did. Because this newest Mariana doesn't listen to reason, apparently.

He helped me rise to my feet and led me over to a set of double doors to the right of the large window. "Sit outside with me. I'll go get us a hot chocolate. Yours with caramel, right?"

It was tempting. Oh, it was tempting. We were looking through the doors onto a 4-season porch with wall-to-wall windows showing a beautiful view of his snowy backyard. I swallowed with difficulty. "Um…"

"We don't even have to talk. Just sit with me, Mariana. We'll just pass the time."

I didn't trust myself to speak, so I just nodded. He must have noticed, as he stepped back. "Go make yourself comfortable. I'll be right out."

When he came back, my breath hitched a little when he sat on the loveseat next to me. There were other seats, but this one looked so soft I couldn't resist. As much as I could see in the dim lighting back here, anyway.

"Your home is lovely," I said, still a little surprised he could afford such a beautiful place on a retail worker's salary. I'd done enough retail work to know how hard it was to make ends meet, unless you were fairly high up the management chain. "How long have you lived here?"

His eyes swung over to meet mine, and he handed me a steaming cup. "I bought this place three years ago." He paused to take a sip. "It's great. But it was an abandoned piece of crap then, so that's how I bought it cheap."

"Oh, so … you fixed it up? You're … wow, the Terry I remember wasn't the do-it-yourself type of guy." I paused, softening my tone. "Not that I knew you very well."

Dammit, why did I bring up the past, especially *that* part of the past? I needed to shut up. I took a sip of the hot drink, which was pure delight on my taste buds and delicious warmth down my throat. I groaned and closed my eyes, savoring it.

Terry coughed. "I guess you like the hot chocolate?"

I smiled as I looked over at him, staring back at me.

My smile wilted though. Too much eye contact. Not a great idea. Especially in ultra-romantic settings.

Once again, what am I doing here?

"So, what brought you back here, to Shipsvold?"

Was this a safe question? I wasn't even sure anymore. I wanted to know what he'd been doing in the past few years. We couldn't avoid it forever. But only for a few years, not far enough back to touch on—

"Needed work, a place to stay, somewhere to get back on my feet after … well, you know." He looked down.

"No, I don't know," I said gently.

"We made some bad investments. Blair's ventures looked really good on paper, but … well, I won't get into all the awful details. It blew up in our faces."

My brow crinkled as I thought about this. "Your sister's ventures? What about yours? You don't strike me as being irresponsible."

A flash of annoyance crossed over his face as he looked at me briefly and then stared out the window. "Aren't we all a bit irresponsible when we're young?" He paused, enough for me to hear the double meaning. "But they were hers. Blair inherited their money. I only got the properties."

"What? Why?"

He sighed. "She was older, and she was always interested in the finance stuff. I had other interests, or maybe I didn't really know what I wanted. In any case, we ended up in debt, so we had to sell the properties too. Leaving us with precisely … nothing."

I mulled this over. "You said 'we' were in debt, but don't you mean *she* was in debt? You sold your properties to clean up *her* mess?"

His head whipped around, and he scowled. "It wasn't like that. She's my sister, the only close family I had … we were a team."

I had clearly struck a nerve. But I pressed on. I had never liked his sister, and I knew she never liked me. She'd always glared at me when he wasn't looking. "But she was older and wiser, so she should've been taking care of you, not the other way around."

He looked out the window again and then sighed. "She did, in some ways. She was there for me when no one else was." He looked at me then briefly, frowning. "During the most difficult times of my life."

I swallowed with some effort. I knew his parents died the same year we met. Was he suggesting … somehow I wasn't there for him? As though I hadn't tried *everything* to get in touch with him? I felt my defenses rise.

And then … I looked over, saw the tilt of his head slightly downward, and I felt his pain.

I shouldn't say anything. Or, I should say something vaguely comforting. Just to be a decent person. Not to dredge up the past. Just keep it light.

"I would've been there for you," I said softly.

Why? Why did I say that? I put my face in my hands.

He scoffed and rose quickly from his seat before striding over to the window.

I didn't know whether to follow him. He seemed almost angry, maybe even volatile. But why would he be?

I probably should give him some space. Definitely should.

"I would have …" I said, rising and then taking a few tentative steps in his direction. "You don't believe me?"

Or maybe comfort from me would've been the last thing he wanted, and I was just embarrassing myself again. I sighed. "Terry?"

He didn't respond at first, but I saw his chest rise and fall heavily as he breathed in and out, gazing out at the wintry landscape. Finally, he said, "I doubt it, but it doesn't matter now."

I walked the last few steps to stand next to him alongside the window. "I can't believe you didn't even *try* though. That you'd just assume …" I shook my head, unable to continue. Had he really had such a low opinion of me? Why? I must have massively misjudged our relationship.

He finally turned to me then, and his eyes were cold as they met mine. "Why would I have tried, Mariana?"

Stricken, I stumbled back. "I … because …" Because I thought we cared about each other. Because I thought we were in love, even. I couldn't tell him any of these things. I didn't understand any of this.

"I knew you'd probably blocked me. And even if you hadn't … well, I wasn't going to be seen as taking advantage of the situation to make you talk to me."

Confusion washed over me, and I felt light-headed. "What?"

He stared at me for what felt like forever as I tried to make sense of his words. I gripped a chair nearby. "I … I need to sit down," I mumbled.

He let out a heavy sigh. "Mariana. I didn't bring you out here to upset you or dredge up the past. We both moved on, long ago. Let's just leave it in the past where it belongs."

I felt a stab of pain in my chest when he said we'd moved on. Maybe he had, but me? No, I obviously hadn't. I had been kidding myself for many years. Sure, I'd dated some, but I'd never fallen in love, not since him. I'd never even wanted to fall in love or … honestly, to feel any strong feelings that had the power to break me like that again.

But why … I had to know. To put this to rest, for good. "Terry, no. I think … well, I need to know something." I waited until he made eye contact again, his expression cautious. "I didn't block you. Why did you think that?"

His eyes searched mine for a moment before he looked

away. "Seriously? What else was I supposed to think?"

I forced myself to keep looking at him and breathe steadily. "Well, considering how often I contacted you, how could you *not* think I wanted to talk to you?" And then I had to ask the question that was burning in my mind, even while I felt my eyes become moist. "And why didn't you meet me at Christmas?"

Chapter 15

I looked at his wide eyes as he exhaled softly. "I was *here*. Like we planned," I continued, hardly caring that a tear was dangerously close to escaping from my eyelid. "I never blocked you, but I did give up after that. How could I not?"

I had to look away for a moment and dabbed at my eyes. When I looked back at him, his jaw had dropped.

He cleared his throat, his eyes intent and never leaving mine. "You're serious," he said slowly.

My brow furrowed, but before I could respond, he held up his hand and placed it briefly on my shoulder. "Mariana, I … I believe you, somehow. But I never got any messages from you."

My eyebrows scrunched together as I took this in. "You never—"

"Ever." I saw his Adam's apple bob as he swallowed hard. "I think we were connected on social media at first, but then you either blocked me or deleted your accounts, I wasn't sure. But emails, texts, calls … you never reached out. I called you all the time, sent you so many messages. I even called the resort eventually, but the manager at the time wouldn't give me any information."

It's a good thing I wasn't the fainting type. My heart was racing and my brain was in overdrive at this news. He believed me. And yet, his experience was the opposite. Somehow, I think I believed him. "What … how—I mean, I don't understand. How is this possible?"

He took both my hands and then looked back up to my

face. "Do you trust me?"

I looked into those gorgeous dark eyes, the ones I'd get lost in every day if I could. I just nodded.

"Good," he said, squeezing my hands gently. "I think … it sounds like you were as desperate to get in touch as I was. And I can't—" he croaked and then cleared his throat. "I don't know what to do with that info. What could've happened? A tech failure?"

I shook my head slowly. "That would only make sense if it were just one medium, but I swear, I was trying everything. Calls, SMS, email, social media. How unlikely is it that tech failures occurred with all of those technologies?"

"*And* we were connecting just fine before I left you," he said thoughtfully. "We texted all the time when I stayed here."

It was dim enough that he probably couldn't see me blush, thankfully. "I remember. It made the laundry shifts less tedious."

He didn't smile, but for the first time since we came out here, I saw a hint of lightness in his expression. But then it disappeared. "OK, then … what could have happened?"

I shook my head, at a total loss. I wasn't that tech savvy, but I was reasonably proficient with communication tools.

We were silent for a long time, both lost in thought. I didn't even notice at first when his thumb started rubbing the back of my hands oh so gently. But then I did notice, and oh … I couldn't think anymore.

Abruptly, he stood up and pulled me up with him and then led me over to where we'd sat before. "I have an idea. Let's check our phones."

I nodded. "Oh, good idea. Why don't you try to call or text me? And I'll try to email you."

"Sure."

"Oh, I suppose you need my number. I haven't changed it, but you probably didn't keep it—"

"I never deleted it," he said, pinning me with a look that was hard to look away from.

"Oh." I looked down at my phone. "I think I have your

email too." Suddenly feeling nervous, I wasn't sure what to say in the email. *I love you and I always have?* Um, no. *Get a hold of yourself, Mariana!* I can just keep it simple. I sent an email with just the word "test" and then waited for him to write me a text.

We both looked up and waited ... and waited. No notifications.

He frowned, as did I. I opened my phone to try to find the blocklist. When I did, I handed my phone to him. "Are any of these your numbers?"

He scanned over the short list. "Nope." He showed his blocklist, which was considerably longer, but I didn't see my number on it.

I leaned back in frustration and crossed my arms. "What the hell? How can this be?" Has my whole life been ruined by a freak technology fail? Well, *whole life* sounds pretty dramatic. Surely that's not—and the denial evaporated as my eyes landed on this man beside me, trying to figure out what had been keeping us apart. My heart soared just a bit, even as I tried to breathe steadily and remind myself we were just clearing things up from the past, not planning a future.

His brows were furrowed as he played with his phone some more. Then he looked up with a pensive expression. "I just remembered, around the time the resort vacation was ending, I was having some trouble with my phone. I can't remember if it was the memory or storage or what. I think my dad and my sister helped me fix it."

"That's ... interesting," I said, feeling a pang of something that felt like a warning. Of what, I wasn't sure. "What made you think of that?"

He leaned back and crossed his legs. "Oh, I was just thinking about how I'd lost our original text history, from when I stayed at the resort. I think they had to clear some space on my phone or something, I can't remember. They were the more tech-savvy ones in the family."

I felt like I was slowly waking up to something, but I wasn't sure what. "You lost our original text history. Well, guess what? So did I. Poof, gone, same timing. I have no idea why. Nobody was using my phone or helping me fix anything. I was actually really heartbroken about it. How ... how could this have happened to both of us?"

Oh my god, what if ...

"Mariana, tell me this," he said, sitting up abruptly and swiping on his phone to his Contacts list again. He handed it to me. "Is that your phone number?"

My eyes traveled downward from his face to the phone with something like reluctance because I suddenly knew what I'd find.

My voice was barely a whisper. "No."

I was shaking as I found his contact info in my phone and presented it to him.

"Goddammit!" he thundered, suddenly jumping to his feet. "Not my number. This is no accident. Someone has screwed with us. Who the hell would—" The blood drained from his face then.

I didn't even have to say anything.

"It couldn't be her," he said weakly. "She would never ..."

"Then who else?" I asked.

He shook his head, over and over. "I don't ... I don't *know*. This is insane, you know? People don't really do things like this, do they? And my own sister ... it's impossible."

"And yet ..." I trailed off. I knew he just had to come to this on his own. If I tried to convince him, he'd want to defend her, and I'd be the bad guy. Maybe. Or maybe there was no other explanation.

"My dad wouldn't have done this. Right? Oh crap, I don't even know anymore." He looked truly crushed. "Even if my dad was in on it, Blair would've probably known. Those two were thick as thieves."

I hesitated before saying this, but it needed to be said. "Well, and there's also the fact that she hated me. Your parents didn't approve of me either."

I couldn't interpret the look on his face then. Maybe

he wanted to defend his family, but he couldn't. Not in this moment. His expression was devastated as he said, "I thought she liked you. But I guess you knew better. So … she had the motive."

"It's almost like a Caroline Bingley situation, but so much more devious. Maybe even illegal," I said, more to myself than to him.

"Caroline who?"

I offered a slight smile. "Never mind. Fictional thing, another time."

He nodded absently. "So what are we going to do?"

I winced. "Well, *I'm* not going to do anything. She's not my sister. I wouldn't even know how to get in touch with her anyway. If you want to confront her, it's up to you."

"Damn right I'll be confronting her. That's putting it nicely." But the sudden rage seemed to dissipate quickly, and he blew out a long breath. "I don't see any possible way we can get over this, honestly. Unless there's some misunderstanding that explains … but how likely is that?"

He looked so sad that I squeezed his shoulder lightly, and he eventually looked over at me. "So you really came for me on Christmas Eve, all those years ago?"

Moment of truth.

I took a deep breath. "I really did. Even though I'd heard nothing from you … for some reason, I still had a little stupid hope."

"Hope isn't stupid," he said softly.

My breath hitched. "It's not?"

He shook his head, his eyes wandering all over my face.

We were only inches apart, and I think one of us leaned in. Maybe both. His face, his lips, so close. His breath on my face. His eyes held mine, and nothing could've taken me away from him, from this moment. Nothing—

Except an irritating phone beep. I jumped back, placing my hand on my chest as my already fast heart rate seemed to double. Disoriented, I watched him fumble for his phone in his pocket and then unlock the screen.

He was silent for a moment as he read and then chuckled, wiping his brow. He typed something in response to the message and then turned it off and looked back at me.

I crossed my arms. "What was that?" I realized how I sounded. And yet ... I had to know, dammit.

"Oh, just a text, wanting to see if I'm home tonight."

My eyebrows must have floated up to my hairline. "Oh, really?"

He rolled his eyes. "Not that kind of text. It was Gram. Making sure I was safe at home from the snow."

I narrowed my eyes. "Your grandma texts you at ..." I looked down at my watch and widened my eyes. How had the time passed so quickly? "Midnight?"

"Well, sometimes. She's a night owl. And it's not just any night, it's Christmas Eve." He grinned.

I wasn't sure whether to believe him, but I nodded warily. "OK, if you say so."

"Mariana, I'm serious." He picked up the phone again and unlocked it before holding it in front of my face. "See?"

I looked at the screen. It was indeed a text conversation with Gram. And she did indeed ask if he was safe from the blizzard. I had to laugh at that. "Blizzard, eh?"

He took the phone back. "She's a bit dramatic at times." He looked me in the eye then and turned to face me again. "Mariana, I wouldn't lie to you. I have plenty of faults, but you can trust me not to lie to you at least." He took a long breath in and out. "OK?"

I swallowed with more effort than usual. It was hard to form words, so I just nodded.

Where do we go from here?

Or maybe ... we don't go anywhere? I shouldn't presume that tonight's revelations change anything. It was a long time ago, and surely he had gotten over me long ago.

But you had that epic kiss...

Eh, so maybe he was attracted to me in that moment, but we were arguing too ... he still doesn't even like me. Probably.

"I can see the wheels turning, Mariana," he said, looking at me steadily.

My eyes shifted to his from where they had wandered to the window. "Ah, sorry. Overactive brain, you know me."

A pensive expression claimed his face. "I'm not sure I do. You've changed in some ways … but not in others. I'm not sure I know you that well anymore."

Once again I was thankful for the dim lighting because I knew my face was on fire at that moment. "Right, you're right," I said, looking down into my lap. How utterly mortifying. He couldn't possibly still be in love with me if he felt like he didn't even know me anymore. I couldn't be the old Mariana anymore, the one he had loved—I'd left her behind. Though every day, more and more, I wondered whether I was neither Mariana LaBelle nor Mariana Northam anymore. I didn't seem to fit anywhere. And why was I thinking about this anyway? It's not like I wanted him to be in love with me … did I? I closed my eyes, trying to shut out all the thoughts.

He looked concerned. "I didn't mean it like that, Mari—"

I forced a smile on my face, one of the most painful ones I'd ever pasted on, which was saying a lot considering I was in the hospitality industry. "I get it, Terry." I moved to sit on the edge of the seat then, as though to rise soon. "So, I don't know about you, but I'm exhausted. Do you have a blanket I could use on the couch?"

"Mariana," he said so slowly that I had to turn and look at him. "Don't run away. We should talk."

I made a loud fake yawn. "I really am tired, Terry. Sorry, can we talk another time?" When he didn't answer, I stood up and looked down at him. "I'll figure out the sleep stuff so you don't have to bother. Shouldn't be too hard to find a blanket somewhere." I gave him a polite smile and turned to leave.

I'd only taken three steps when his heavy hand fell on my shoulder, stopping me in my tracks. I sighed and pivoted to face him. "Yes?"

He looked at me silently for so long that I almost turned

around and left, but just before I gave up waiting, he spoke quietly. "I'll help you get comfortable."

I nodded, swallowing the lump in my throat. "Thanks."

"I could take the couch if you want to sleep in my room," he said, his eyes darker than ever in the dim light. "But knowing you, you'll stubbornly insist on the couch."

I pursed my lips. "I'm not *stubborn*. But yes, I'm perfectly fine on the couch. If you'll just help me find a blanket, I can use one of the throw pillows." I spun on my heel then and left him standing there, but I could still hear his loud sigh behind me.

Chapter 16

The next morning, as I slowly opened my eyes, all I could see through my lashes was red and gold. I closed my eyes, realizing I must still be asleep, in some fanciful dream.

Music. A song with ... bells.

The smells—oh, the smells.

Peppermint, gingerbread, fire.

Wait, what? *Fire*?

My eyes flew open, and I threw off the covers as I frantically rubbed the sleep out of my eyes.

Oh. A fireplace.

Not danger.

I exhaled heavily and fell back down into the cushions, taking the blanket with me. Someone had started a fire. It was cozy and warm. No big—

Wait, what? Someone ... who—where—oh crap, I'm at Terry's house.

My eyes were wide open now and racing around the room, or what I could see of it from my frozen position on the couch.

He had been decorating? Baking? Starting a fire ... There were even stockings hung on the fireplace. Two of them, actually, one red and one green. The music, it was *Carol of the Bells*, one of my favorites. I didn't see any food, so the smells must have been candles.

My heart must have skipped a beat or several as I slowly sat and swung my legs toward the floor, my mouth agape.

I half expected to see some holiday socks or slippers

waiting for me on the floor, but alas, the floor was clear around me. I covered a yawn and patted my unruly hair down before rising to my feet. I turned to glance behind me and had to steady myself. I must have gasped audibly because then I heard footsteps from somewhere down the hall.

He was coming—he … he got a Christmas tree? I stared at the gorgeous fir, strung with soft gold and red lights, beads, and bulbs, with shiny silver icicles.

"Hey."

I tore my eyes away from the beautiful tree to stare at him in wonder. "You—you—what …"

He looked amused as he leaned against the doorway frame. "Cat got your tongue, my sweet?"

I blinked several times, my heart pounding. "Uh, I'm not —"

He laughed then, a throaty sound that caught me off guard. He seemed relaxed, different than I'd seen him since … well, back then. "Merry Christmas, Mariana."

I swallowed, trying but failing to take a steady breath. "Terry, what—what is all this? You …" I looked at my watch. "It's only 8:30. How early did you get up?"

He smiled and shook his head. "Doesn't matter. Do you like it?"

"I—of course I like it." I swept my hands around and whispered, "It's beautiful, I can't believe it. How … I mean, how did you get a Christmas tree in here at the last minute? And you decorated it too—"

"Mariana," he said, clearly trying not to laugh. "I literally live on a Christmas tree farm, remember? That's where we are, right now."

I slammed my palm into my forehead. "Of course, I forgot." I made eye contact again, this time with a more serious expression. "But all this—this had to have taken you *hours*." I waited, and he didn't dispute this. "Why would you … why?"

He shrugged slightly and looked at the tree briefly before looking back at me. "Because I knew you'd like it. You love

Christmas."

"For—for me?" I squeaked. My eyes darted away, only to land on a single wrapped present beneath the tree. I don't know how I missed seeing it before. It was small and square, immaculately wrapped in shiny green and silver striped paper. I pointed to it. "Oh my god, what's that?"

He took a few slow steps toward me. "Sorry, it's only one. I didn't have much lead time. Shall we sit?" He extended his arm outward toward the tree.

I should've probably said *No* or *What the hell is going on?* But I sat down beside him in front of the gorgeous tree, marveling at the beautiful ornaments. They looked older but well preserved. Probably expensive at one time.

When he placed the small present in my hands, I realized my hands were shaking and hoped he didn't notice. "Um, I don't have a gift for you," I mumbled.

He laughed, dispelling a bit of the tension. "Of course you don't. It would be weird if you did, I think." He nodded toward the gift. "Go on, open it."

The present in my hands was light. I removed the wrap carefully and then opened the box. Inside was a small sheet of paper.

I looked up at him and raised my eyebrows in question. The look on his face caught me off guard a bit. For the first time this morning, he looked slightly ill at ease … uncomfortable. Nervous?

Opening the note, I read it aloud, "Mariana, will you go out with me?" I dropped the note, shocked.

Before I could even begin to think about what to say, his deep voice rumbles close to my ear. "I hear there's a really good seafood place down at the Breakers Alehouse."

A shiver went through me, and all I could do was breathe in and out.

My voice was but a whisper. "That's … we … " He remembered this? We went to Breakers on our first date. We both ordered fish and chips, and I remember teasing him about how rich boys were supposed to have fancier taste in food.

He waited patiently while I tried to process this, which was impossible because how the hell could I process something like this? My brain and my heart and my body were all screaming at me a thousand different things, and all I could do was try to breathe. Finally, I made eye contact with him. Terry, of the deep dark eyes, the smile I think I'd do anything for. And I wanted nothing more than to melt in his arms.

In fact, I started to slump to the side a bit, as he put his hands on my shoulders abruptly. "Woah there," he said, sounding concerned. "Why don't we get you set up on the couch over there. I'll get a blanket, and we'll get cozy by the fire."

Nodding, I didn't resist when he took my hands to help me to my feet. I did feel a little lightheaded. "I'm a bit thirsty, actually."

"Say no more," he said. After tucking a soft blanket around me on the couch, he left, but not for long. Soon, he was before me with a tray of deliciousness set on the coffee table in front of us. He sat down next to me and handed me a glass of water first. "I have coffee and hot cocoa. And of course, some Christmas morning treats. Sugar cookies, a cheese ball and crackers if you're more interested in something savory—"

"Terry, it looks amazing. Seriously, when did you have time to do all this?" I looked at him in awe.

He shook his head with a wry grin. "I'll never tell." He sat silently and watched me drink some water and then try a sugar cookie, which was delicious. "Yes, I made them. Don't look so surprised that I'm a man of many talents. Old family recipe." He smiled but then looked serious. "So, about the note. What do you say?"

"I say … I don't know, Terry. It's so sudden. I need to think—"

His lips curved into a deep frown. "Is it that sudden though? I still have feelings for you, Mariana," he said, his voice sounding a bit choked. "I think—no, I *know* you feel something too."

I can't look away, his expression is so raw, so honest. I can't speak though.

"Mariana, please. Just admit that, at least." He paused, hesitation in his eyes. "Or—or tell me if I've misread everything."

I nod, closing my eyes briefly. "I do feel something for you." My voice was soft, but I knew he heard me because relief washed over his face. But only briefly, before I continued, "You need me to be honest, so how can I … I don't even know what is the truth. I don't know what I want. You want Mariana LaBelle, but she doesn't exist anymore. I am not her, Terry. *She's* the girl you loved, and she's gone. I can't be her, not for you, not for anyone."

So many emotions passed over his face—confusion, pain, fear, disappointment, sadness, and then anger. "You don't get to tell me what I want, Mariana. I want you." His jaw was tense as he pierced me with his gaze. "You—you're not making sense. There's one Mariana. It's you."

I spoke slowly, "I have changed. I built a new life for myself—"

"Yes, but you're still you, the girl I—"

"No," I said firmly. "I'm not. I built a new me. That's why I changed my name." I couldn't read his expression then but kept going shakily. "I—I can imagine it's hard to understand. But trust me, I'm so much happier with the new me, my new life—so much shame I left behind."

I wanted to add that being around him had made me question everything, that I didn't really know who I was anymore, but it hurt to even admit that to myself, much less say it aloud. Instead, I just stared at him, my heart aching as he looked down at his hands.

He opened his mouth several times to speak and then stopped. The slump of his shoulders told me everything I needed to know.

And I realized what I had to do. "Terry, one thing hasn't changed. The old Mariana was head over heels for you." I took a deep breath. "And the new me … well, you're all I think about.

You've found a—a place in my heart so deep that it's the one part of me I couldn't change, that I think maybe will never change."

One moment, I was peering at him through my tears, and the next, I couldn't breathe. He'd swept me into his arms, and I was suddenly planted in his lap as our lips molded together. Not a slow, sweet, exploratory kiss, but a deep, breathless one that left me clawing at his shirt and gasping for air when his lips moved to kiss my jaw and then travel downward. When his mouth moved over the pounding pulse in my neck, I mumbled something, lacing my fingers through his hair and pulling him closer as I realigned our mouths. I couldn't get enough. It was 10 years of no Terry, of never expecting to feel this again. I couldn't breathe, but I didn't want to. Nothing mattered but this. Nothing.

"Ahh!" His entire body jolted, and he looked with wild eyes toward the floor.

Dazed, I scrambled off him. "What is it?"

He bent down and then sat back, chuckling. "I think you kicked over the hot cocoa, my foot is soaked now." At my horrified expression, he added, "Don't worry, it's not hot anymore. So, is that your thing now? In the throes of passion, you always kick your legs out? First it was the tree in the ballroom…" He stopped then, noticing my expression. "Mariana, it's—I was just joking. It's fine."

I nodded fast, repeatedly. "Yeah, I know. I'm so sorry. I'll clean it up right away if you tell me where your cleaning supplies are?" I started to stand, but he took one of my hands.

"Mariana, stop. Breathe. It's not a big deal, at all."

I breathed in and out. "Still, I should clean up."

He grinned. "I can think of things I'd rather do with you. Far more important than any mess."

Oh my god, what must he think of me? This is—no wonder he's falling for me again. I'm acting like the old Mariana. I have to put a stop to this, *Now*.

With panic coursing through my veins, I let go of his hand roughly and stood up. "I really should be going. But I can clean this up for you first. I am so terribly sorry. This is simply unacceptable—"

He stared at me like I'd grown a third—or fourth—head. "Listen to me. I don't care about the mess. I care about *you*. I want *you*. Not you from the past. I want your present, your future. We can light this room on fire for all I care. I just want you."

As he spoke, the panic started to subside. My eyes filled with tears, and they were running down my cheeks when I sat next to him again.

"Just let me hold you," he said, stretching his arms around my shoulders, which were shaking as I sobbed.

When my breathing started to slow, I pulled back just enough to look at him. "Terry, you—I'm—" I choked out.

"Shhh, it's OK, Mariana. All OK." His expression was gentle as he tried to pull me back in.

"No, I … you need to know. I—I thought I had it all together, the new Mariana did, or so I thought … but lately … well, the truth is, I'm a *mess*, Terry. You don't want all this. Trust me, you don't want me."

I don't know what I expected, but I wasn't prepared for his glower. "Can I decide what I want?"

I bit my lip. "But you don't *know*—"

"Then *let me* get to know you!" He threw his hands up, leaning away from me. "You are such a maddening woman." He exhaled in frustration, looking away for a long moment. "But I want you, all of you. The maddening parts too. And the messy parts. New, old, whatever. We all change, you know? You're not the only one whose life has changed dramatically in the last decade."

I opened my mouth to reply, and I couldn't find the words at first. Of course, his life had changed too, and not for the better. His parents had died, and he'd gone from ridiculously wealthy to … poor? Middle class? I didn't even know his status, but it was certainly massively downgraded from what it was. But he was still the same person, wasn't he? He hadn't needed to change who he was, to discard his old self, his past … that was the difference between us. Maybe what he went through was worse though. I shook my head, more confused than ever. "I don't know," I said hesitantly. "I want everything to be as simple as that, to just … be with you."

Before I could say more, he took both my hands and brought them to his lips as his eyes pierced my soul. "Then it will be simple. Be with me."

I was going to cry again. This man.

I leaned in to kiss him but then stopped, suddenly hearing *Joy to the World*.

"Dammit." His voice was rough as we sat up, looking for our phones. "I'll put it on silent."

I spotted the phone at the same time he did. His eyes slid over to me, probably hoping I hadn't seen it. But I had.

Jane was calling.

Jane.

Another reason we'd been at odds.

I crossed my arms over my stomach, steeling myself for this conversation. Was he going to continue to sabotage me with Jane, as he had been? Could I forgive him for that?

He didn't answer the call but sent it to voicemail and stared into the fireplace for what felt like an eternity.

"I guess we should talk about this," he said, his voice sounding kind of distant. Not warm and comforting as before. I felt my guard go up further, wondering what he was going to say.

"Absolutely," I said firmly, and he turned to look at me. I was all business now, and I lifted my chin as I said, "So have you been working against me with Jane in this business deal?"

He looked back to the fire. "No." A muscle tensed in his jaw. "Also, yes."

I waited for a moment as my ire rose. "Which is it?" I snapped.

His eyes swung toward me, and I was taken aback. He looked sad. Scared. Maybe even defeated. "I'd never try to hurt you. You should know that."

I stuck my chin out, trying to breathe steadily. "Having a

hard time believing it, based on how this conversation is going. But keep going."

He sighed heavily. "When you first started talks with Jane, she was impressed with you. She was really considering it. You had a good shot."

I nodded. "I felt that. And then, something changed." I narrowed my eyes. "What happened?"

He took a deep breath, looking at me only briefly before looking down at his hands. "My grandma convinced her not to sell and … to give it to me instead."

My jaw dropped. "*What?* Why on earth—"

"My grandma is married to Jane. They decided it was best to keep it in the family." He looked at me then, fear and something else in his eyes. Regret?

"Married … is *Nina* your grandma?" He nodded ever so slightly, his expression full of guilt. "That's—why didn't anyone tell me this?"

"I'm sorry, Mariana. Really, we should've—"

"It's a little late for apologies now, isn't it? You let me waste my time and everyone else's trying to woo her … make a fool of myself, really. How … how could you?" I was furious but somehow also on the verge of tears. I had to lean in to the anger to avoid crying *again*. "And how could *they?*"

"I'm sorry," he repeated. "It's not like you and I were on good terms. And they wanted me to wait before telling you."

My eyes widened. "Why? Because it was entertaining for them?"

His eyes hardened. "My grandma isn't like that." But his face softened quickly. "I don't know why. They can be pretty formidable when they're together. I … well, I should've questioned it, I guess. I am sorry."

My tone was bitter, and my throat felt like bile. "Yeah, you should've."

"Please, Mariana. Forgive me. I am truly sorry."

The pleading look in his eyes gave me pause. "Terry, I can't—"

"Please. I know we can work past this. I just … I love you."

And I lost all ability to think. My vision blurred as a fresh round of tears filled my eyes, and my lip shook as I tried to answer, "Terry … I don't know …"

He came to me then and gently wiped my tears with his thumbs. "Please."

I sniffled and then nodded. "I can forgive you. That's not … that's not the issue."

He kissed me softly and then led me back to the couch so we could sit side by side. "Then what is it?"

"I mean, isn't it obvious? Our goals are in direct conflict."

He tilted his head in question. "I want to be with you. I think you want to be with me. Same goals." He offered a small smile as he squeezed my hand.

My eyes flickered with annoyance. "Business goals, Terry. Life goals? I mean, I have other goals in life besides romance. I mean, romance wasn't even a goal at all for me until tonight."

"Business … right." He let go of my hands slowly and scratched the side of his face, which was a bit stubbly. "We wouldn't let that come between us though, right? I wouldn't."

I threw my hands up in the air. "How can you say that? We already have! It's already come between us. It *is* between us. We both want the same thing, and we can't both have it."

The corners of his mouth turned sharply downward as he leaned back against the couch. He sighed heavily. "I didn't know … it's *that* important to you?"

My lips were pressed in a thin line. "It's important to me. Surely you don't expect me to just give up all my life goals for you?" His brow furrowed, but before he could respond, I added, "Are you planning to give yours up for me?"

He stared into the fireplace, his lips firmly shut. Finally, he looked at me with such pain that I flinched. "I see your point. I would not want you to give up your dreams."

I forced myself to nod, even though I wanted to disagree and say I was wrong, that we must find a way, that love can always find a way. But he was right. We had to be mature adults about this. We wanted different things. Well, to be more precise, we wanted the same thing, but only one of us could have it.

It could only end in heartbreak.

And *that* I can't do. Not again.

"I won't survive a painful breakup when this all blows up," I said, fighting back tears. I took a steadying breath. "Once was too many times for me."

He just sat there, slumped on the couch, nodding slowly. He didn't look at me, even when I stood up.

"I'm, uh, just going to get my things. I'll call an Uber, OK?"

He turned toward me then, not getting up from the couch. "I can drive you," he said, sounding dazed.

"No, it's fine. I think it's best … you stay and I go."

He simply nodded and looked in the other direction as I moved behind the couch to grab some things I'd left there.

"Terry, thank you for all this. I'm … so sorry this can't work out." Before he could respond, I fled from the room, grabbing my coat and boots and flying out the front door as fast as possible. I got out my phone to get the Uber, shivering and feeling grateful he had a covered front porch at least. I didn't trust myself to wait inside for his response. He'd make me stay, and it would hardly take anything to convince me. I needed to be strong. I couldn't be with him, even if every piece of my heart screamed at me to go back, to find a way to make it work. My head told me no. The voice of reason, calm, logic. The one that had steered me right all these years. My brain would help me get over him, once again. My heart could not be trusted.

Chapter 17

I saw her walk over—OK, more like strut—to the front desk just as I'd finished downing another huge bottle of water. I'd cried for hours when I got home, and I was hoping the massive quantities of water would combat the dehydrated puffy eye look I was sporting. But I forgot about that the moment I spotted this vile woman.

She was smirking at my new front desk clerk, who looked overwhelmed at the check-in computer. I grabbed a tube of lipstick from my pocket, applied some (it's a power move, don't ask), and walked over. "Can I be of assistance?"

Blair flipped her long blonde hair over her shoulder and laughed. "Well, I hope someone can, because this girl seems confused. I need—" That was the moment where she looked up and saw me. She blinked in recognition, and her face morphed in an instant. "Oh my gosh, if it isn't Maria. So nice to see you," she said in a syrupy sweet voice, holding out a hand that I ignored. "You're the manager now, you said?"

"It's Mariana." I didn't bother to correct her on the manager thing. I was the acting manager right now, as I'd let the other managers go early to celebrate the rest of the holiday evening. I turned to the front desk employee. "Triveni, what seems to be the problem?"

"Well, she wants a room, but we're all booked. She asked if we had rooms set aside for special guests—"

I turned to her. "We do indeed. Are you a special guest, Blair?" I keep my face arranged in an innocent expression.

She gave me a look as though we had an insider thing between us. "Oh, you know I am, we go way back. This girl didn't seem to get it."

I tapped my fingernails on the counter, pretending to think about it. "We do indeed go way back. Way back, I think, 10 years, right?" She smiled at me before flashing a condescending look at poor Triveni. I leveled a serious look at her. "Tell me, Blair, why did you do it?"

She tilted her head, scrunching her penciled eyebrows in confusion. "Why did I do what?"

I repeated myself, this time with a deadly cold tone. "Why did you do it?"

The pretense left her face then, replaced by growing panic. "I don't know what you're accusing me of, but—"

"Yes, you do. Just tell me why, and I'll consider letting you stay here tonight." I wouldn't, but she would find that out soon enough.

She seemed to contemplate this for a moment and then scoffed. "You can't stop me from getting a room here. I don't have to tell you a damn thing."

I raised an eyebrow. "You think?"

She crossed her arms over her chest, pursing her lips. "Let me talk to a different manager. Or your supervisor."

"It's not your lucky day, Blair. Because guess what? I own this place. And it'll be a cold day in hell before you ever stay in my resort." I took a breath, my chest heaving. "Now get out."

Her jaw dropped, and loathing filled her eyes. "You can't just kick me out! I've a right to a room like anyone else."

"I can kick you out, and I will." I pulled out my phone then and called security.

"Why are you here anyway?"

She glared at me, obviously trying to think of another plan of either getting her way or attacking me.

But I held up my hand to stop her. "Let me guess, Terry told you that you aren't welcome at the family Christmas this year? Or maybe your grandma did? Gee, that's too bad, Blair. I can't say you didn't deserve it though."

I don't know what was more satisfying, telling her off or seeing a security guard escort her out the doors as I cheerily waved goodbye.

As soon as she left, I caught Triveni staring at me in wonder. For a moment, I thought it was fear, but she high-fived me with a huge smile. I had to smile back. Employees never gave me high-fives. To each other, sure, but never to me. I just didn't have that kind of relationship with the staff.

I frowned, wondering if the staff saw me as cold or boring or ... I needed to stop thinking like this. As I walked down to the kitchen to get a snack before doing some rounds to check on other areas, I found myself wiping away more tears. Dammit, I can't cry again. I thought I'd at least have the satisfaction from the Blair encounter to buffer against the sadness for a couple hours. But that triumph lasted all of five minutes. After cutting up the apple, I ate two pieces and threw it away. My stomach told me it was time to eat, but I couldn't. Everything tasted like nothing ... everything but the salt of my tears. But I can't live on that, can I? Ugh, deranged thoughts—what's next?

I'd somehow fallen asleep in the managers' office when my phone started ringing with a call. With bleary eyes that were now extremely puffy and dry, I saw Hazel's name and debated whether to answer.

But we always talked on Christmas, even when she hadn't known it was my favorite holiday.

"Hazel, merry Christmas! How are you?"

"Besides meeting the love of my life and finding out he lives in Australia? I'm just fine and dandy," she said sarcastically. "But hey, Merry Christmas!" She puts on happy-go-lucky tone, but it's obviously a front.

"Woah, wait a minute, you didn't mention anyone last night when we talked." Since Hazel was a total romantic, this seemed like kind of a big deal. She was always hoping to find the *one* but always striking out. Like many people in today's modern dating world, I guess. That's why I was glad to stay far, far away from it. Yep, that's why.

"I think it was after that," she said absently. "Anyway, he's Japanese American, only recently moved to Australia for some really good job, but he was here visiting friends. You know I can always tell by the first date or two whether someone is going to work out. Well, yeah. This guy would *work out*, Mari. He would. If he didn't live on the other side of the damn Pacific! I am so goddamn mad. You have no idea."

"I can see that. It's—"

"But more than that—" She started sniffling. "More than that, my heart is broken. *Shattered*. I think I'm going to be done with dating and love forever. And he ... he pretty much said the same. We only have one more day together."

"Oh, Haz. So sorry."

I felt for her, I really did.

But.

They've known each other for one day?

Hmm, OK.

"I know you don't believe in love and all that," she said between full-on sobs now. "But trust me, this guy was *it* for me. I ... I fear I'll never find this again. But I can't imagine moving to another country."

I understood this about her. She'd moved a lot, including living in several countries, as a child and had come into adulthood with a craving to stay in one place. The job she currently had satisfied her need for travel with her need to live in one place—anywhere, really, as long as she could stay put. "I know, but—"

"He proposed," she blurted out.

"Wait, what?"

"Yeah, I know it sounds crazy, but that's the thing ... it didn't feel crazy at all. I just ... it's the distance thing."

Uh, it all sounded crazy, honestly. But I tried to go with it. "That's so sweet. But you said no ... right?"

"I said I had to think about it, but the look in his eyes ... his gorgeous eyes, it was like the light went out. He knows I don't want to move." She stopped, and it sounded like she was blowing her nose. "Sorry, if I keep talking about this, I will just cry the whole time, and then I won't be able to show my face to anyone later."

"Is that …" I tried to choose my words carefully, sensing how fragile she was. "Maybe that's for the best? It's late, and it sounds like you're emotionally exhausted. You should rest."

"I'm meeting him in his room in a half hour. If I have so little time left with my soulmate, I'm not going to waste it sleeping," she said disdainfully. "Have you forgotten what it's like to be in love?"

I sighed, probably a little too loudly. "No, but I wish I had."

Her tone softened. "Really?"

I debated about whether to tell her. She wasn't in a great place right now. I'd never seen her this heartbroken, and I had watched her struggle with dating for years. But maybe some commiseration would help? As much as I hated the idea of sharing, I would have to do it eventually. Perhaps it would help her to feel less alone in her heartbreak.

"Uh, yeah, Terry and I," I managed to say. I stopped to clear my throat. "We almost got back together, actually. We were snowed in last night at his house."

She made a whooping sound. "*What*? I hope you're planning to give me every detail, including how big—"

I chuckled despite my embarrassment. "Oh, not like that. We only kissed and talked … and talked some more. He—he said he wanted to be with me." I swallowed the massive lump in my throat.

"Wow, I figured he was still into you, but I'm kind of surprised he just went for it."

Puzzled, I frowned. "If you thought that, why would it be surprising?"

"Well, because it's you and …" she trailed off, suddenly sounding uncertain.

"And? What about me?" I probably sounded a bit defensive, expecting the worst.

"I mean, you're a little intimidating sometimes. That's all. It's fine, Mari," she said lightly.

"I—what—never mind," I said, blowing out a breath to gain some control of my firing emotions. "Anyway, I found out Nina is his grandma. Can you believe it?" I heard her gasp on the other line. "Yeah, I was shocked too. And that's why Jane's not looking to sell … because they want it to stay in the family, apparently through Terry."

"Oh wow, I did not see that coming. Still, I guess it explains a lot." Her tone was so nonchalant that I wondered if she truly understood what this meant for us. "So back to you and Terry … you said you *almost* got together. What stopped you?"

Wasn't it obvious?

"Uh, I mean, the business thing—"

"Well, yeah, it's a wrinkle in your plans, but what's the real reason? Is it because you just couldn't forgive him for what happened 10 years ago? For ghosting you?"

I groaned. "No. But about that, it turns out, he didn't really ghost me. He did everything he could to contact me, but—you've got to humor me for a minute here because this is going to sound like it's straight out of a soap opera or something—his awful older sister sabotaged us. She switched our phone numbers and set up social media blocks and who knows what else. It might've actually been his sister *and* his dad since apparently they were both pretty tech-savvy and neither one of them liked me. But since his parents died, I didn't want to suggest his dad might've played a role. Just knowing it wasn't him—that he never wanted us to end … well, it's enough. Plus, I got her uppity self hauled out by security earlier when she tried to book a room here. It was amazing."

I heard a shocked puff of air. "Mari! Oh my god, such drama, I can't believe I'm missing it all. And he didn't … oh, he was just as heartbroken as you were when your summer fling didn't continue—oh, I—" she stopped, returning to sobbing. "I can't, Mari, it's like my heart has been broken twice tonight, once for me and once for you."

"Aww, Hazel, I know the feeling. My heart aches for you. But don't worry about me. I'll be fine, just like I have been for the past 10 years," I assured her in my confident tone.

A short laugh erupted from her. "Oh, OK."

My lips curled into a frown. "What?"

"Have you—" She stopped then and was silent for a few seconds. "Never mind. Anyway, so you still haven't told me, why aren't you and Terry getting together now?"

I felt my heart in my throat, and I couldn't speak for a moment. Finally, I managed to say, "I just can't."

"What do you mean you can't? Why not?"

I inhaled and exhaled slowly. "We're not compatible. Our business goals aren't compatible. And I'm not the same person he fell in love with. It's … it would never work."

She was quiet for a moment. "But you love him, don't you?"

I swallowed, willing the tears not to fall yet again. "I do."

"And he loves you?"

"I … he said he did." But he doesn't know what he's saying. He loves the person I used to be, not the one I am now, not the one I want to be.

"Then the rest shouldn't matter," she said softly. "You can make it work. It will be worth it, and you'll see—"

"No. The rest *does* matter," I said, a bit too forcefully. Then, more softly, I said, "It matters to me."

"More than love?" When I didn't answer, she let out a long, frustrated-sounding sigh. "Mari, you can have love, be with the one you love. He—he's right there. You don't have to move halfway across the damn world and give up your life to be with him. He's right there. Willing to love you. And you're saying no?"

When she put it that way, it sounded like I was doing something wrong. I bristled, "Just because he lives here doesn't mean this is right for my life."

She scoffed. "But you'll never know, will you? Because you won't even try."

I swallowed, clenching my fists. "Hazel, that's not fair."

"No, Mari," she said, a note of bitterness in her voice that I'd almost never heard. "What's not fair is that you found the one, and he's right there in front of you. But you think you can't have it. Yet I found the one, and he's … it's impossible …" Her voice became muffled, and I could tell she was crying again.

"Hazel," I pleaded, "let's not compare. I know what I'm doing. Your situation—"

"I have to go now," she said quickly, sniffling. "I can't hear this. Don't—don't call me for a while. I need a break."

Then the call ended.

My eyes were wide as I stared at the phone in shock and then set it down in front of me. I can't remember when we'd ever fought before. Well, there was that one time in grad school, but we'd been drinking. And a couple of small spats about resort business, but nothing serious, nothing very personal. Nothing like this.

There was only one thing to do. I put my head on my desk and cried.

It seemed I had an endless supply of tears today.

Chapter 18

After too many days spent on the couch wallowing, I'd had enough. I was not a wallower.

I looked and smelled gross, as did my living room, kitchen, and bedroom, where I'd spent … how many days was it? Three or four, maybe. Possibly five. I'd gone off the grid except in the most dire emergencies, and only my general manager and top advisors were allowed to contact me. No one did. I think they were afraid.

But no more.

This wasn't me.

I felt so much better after driving to the salon for my usual highlights. The resort had an expensive salon on the premises, but I preferred to keep a low profile when it came to personal care.

I skipped the grocery store though. I knew better than to go where Terry shops again—I was using the delivery service from now on.

Then, as I drove closer to the large parking lot, there he was.

Terry was loading trees into a massive truck. Probably the same trees we'd set up together. I thought about the moment of passion we'd shared and then had to swerve before almost driving into a snowbank.

What am I going to say? Oh my god, I was not at all prepared to see him again. I mean, I had known that I *would* at some point. But I wasn't ready … I didn't have a strategy yet.

After I parked, I was slow to turn off the car, unbuckle my seat belt, put my visor up, and eventually open my car door. I took a deep breath before stepping out of the car as I steeled myself for the awkwardness and pain to come, while also feeling still a bit of that usual excitement about just getting to see him.

I needn't have bothered.

He'd just finished and was already driving away. As he shifted from reverse to forward, I was sure he spotted me, but he gave no indication. He merely turned his head and left.

I should've felt only relief, but instead, I felt hollow. I forced my legs to trudge through the snow to the entrance. I usually parked at a side entrance closer to where my rooms were, but I wasn't thinking clearly when I pulled in. Oh well, I'd move my car later, probably. Maybe.

As I walked through the automatic doors, fluffing my hat after taking it off, I noticed my eyes were dry, at least. Good, the last thing I needed was for more staff to see me teary-eyed. I'm sure they'd witnessed quite the show last week when I'd had the Christmas meltdown of all meltdowns.

I gave a friendly wave to the front desk person, who I didn't know very well. The moment she saw me, her eyes widened, and she started waving her arm fast. I guess she wanted me to come over?

I sighed. I just wanted to get back to my room so I could wallow some more—just a bit more, since I was not really a wallower, of course. But instead I smiled and walked over to the desk, where the employee was talking to a tall blonde woman who looked … well, expensive. As most of our guests do.

I slid behind the front desk and looked at Lanie, as indicated by her employee nametag. "Hi Lanie, I'm Mariana. I don't think we've met yet, but it's nice to meet you. Can I help with something?"

Lanie fidgeted. "I—yeah, yes, it's nice to meet you. Um, yes, there's a guest here claiming to…"

I didn't hear the rest of what she said because my head had started to turn to face the guest on the other side of the desk.

And when I saw her, I stopped thinking, stopped hearing.

Stopped breathing.

Finally, I gasped. I couldn't even begin to physically form words, even if I could think of which ones to use.

What words could possibly fit this moment?

"Mariana, it is you," she said in soft, measured tones.

I still couldn't speak. I heard Lanie say something behind me, but it didn't register. I just kept staring.

Upon closer inspection, the woman's hair had a bit of strawberry blonde, but it was extremely subtle and cut short in a chic, expensive cut. She was around the same height and build as me. Her nose was small, her cheekbones high. Her face and eyes so familiar, with faint lines in the corner of her eyes and mouth. And on her face was my polite, gracious smile.

"M—m—" I couldn't say it. I couldn't. So many thoughts and feelings were zipping through my brain and my body that I had to brace my hands on the counter to steady myself. I took a couple of steadying breaths, reminding myself I'm Mariana Northam, dammit. I don't get intimidated or overcome by feelings or any of that nonsense. It's time to be a Northam once again. Not the person she probably thinks I am.

When I knew I could handle myself, I raised my eyes back to her face, which was looking at me curiously. "My mother, I presume?" I asked.

That smile again. The gracious one, the one I used at work, mostly. Often when I didn't want to be smiling at all. "Yes, Mariana. I am your mother."

"Oh," I said, giving her the same smile back as I patted my straight, light blonde hair. At least it wasn't strawberry-blonde anymore, like hers. I'd been dyeing it for years. "Pleased to meet you. Can I help you with something?"

A flash of something—irritation maybe, or perhaps even hurt—passed over her face at my blunt question, but she smiled again. "I came to introduce myself and get to know you, darling."

Darling? Is she serious?

She can't be.

I wonder if she wants money or something. Though it certainly doesn't look like it, from her expensive outfit and luggage.

Still, why else would she be here?

"*Mother*, how did you know I was here?" I asked, gritting my teeth through a false smile. "Seeing as how we'd never met or spoken before."

"Oh, I have friends in high places," she said with a laugh that sounded more like a cackle. "They tracked you down through the foster system and then to that family that bequeathed you their fortune. Rhonda Johnson, I think was her name?"

I closed my eyes briefly. "Ah. Rhonda *Jackson*." She'd bitterly resented me since the settlement from Lisa was announced. She couldn't believe her mother had let me inherit even a penny, much less a sizeable fortune. I'd tried to reason with her and make amends, but she'd wanted nothing to do with me. What sweet revenge this must be for her, telling my mother my whereabouts. She knew what this would mean for me.

And what did it mean?

That was the worst part … because I didn't know.

"I must say, I'm impressed that you've made something of yourself. Given your past and the reprehensible conditions your father raised you in …" She shook her head, her lips curled in distaste. "Well, it's satisfying to know you turned out more like me after all." She waved her arms around, pointing to the scene around us, literally a place of luxury.

I inhaled sharply. She couldn't possibly be …

No, she was. She was blaming Dad!

I attempted to keep my voice calm as I replied, "The reprehensible conditions my father raised me in … you mean because he was sick and therefore poor?" She raised her eyebrows a hair, but I continued as my face went cold. "Don't you dare look down on my father, who only did his best. What did *you* do?"

Her lips were thin, and her polite smile was back. Why?

Was this really a time to smile? Does this woman have no heart?

"It was not ideal or timely for me—"

Yeah, she had no heart.

My laugh was brittle. "You're serious? Having a child to support wasn't timely? Well, guess what? You could've tried. Even a little."

Her eyes widened for a brief moment and then returned to the flat globes from before. "Mariana, please, let's be civil. I didn't come here to argue. I want us to know each other—"

"What about what I want? Does that not matter?"

"Well, of course, darling," she purred, "And I know every girl wants her mother."

"I did," I confessed. "I did want a mother. More than anything." My voice broke. "But I don't want you. You're not a mother." Her sharp intake of breath only propelled me further. "Well, maybe you're somebody's mother, but you're not mine."

"Mariana, you don't mean that," she said, reaching out to pat my hand. I pulled it back quickly and felt her manicured nails scrape over my skin. "I know this is a surprise, but I'm confident you'll recover quickly. Being emotional isn't your style, is it, darling? I could see it when I walked in. You were so cool, calm, sophisticated. You're like me, darling."

My jaw dropped.

"No. *No.* I don't want to be like you." I was nearly panting now, and I didn't even care. "Anything but that." This time I saw some emotion on her face, but it didn't look like hurt. More like anger. "Go. I don't want to see you. Now, or ever."

I spun on my heel then and walked away. Just as she did 29 years ago.

Chapter 19

I'd already sunk deep into the couch beneath my favorite blanket—a curious numb feeling settling over me, or maybe shock?—when the doorbell rang. I groaned loudly.

Now what? I'd forgotten to put my Do Not Disturb sign on my door and on my phone/email message system. I stomped over to the door and threw it open, ready to get rid of whoever was bothering me.

My eyes went wide as they landed on her.

Hazel's long hair was in a messy bun, and she was wearing faded red sweats and an old t-shirt that looked like they needed a good wash. "Mari, can I come in?"

I nodded, moving aside and then shutting the door after her.

"Peace offering?" She was standing there holding out a bakery takeout bag with a sheepish smile.

I took the bag and looked inside. Scones. Cinnamon chip, my favorite. "You didn't need to bring anything. Come here." Then I hugged her. Really, really hugged her.

And then I jumped back because … ew. "Um, Haz, when did you last wash that shirt?"

She pulled it toward her nose. "Uh, good question."

I smiled and pointed behind me. "It's all right. As you can see, my place is a bit of a mess too. It turns out I'm a wallower after all."

"Duh." She rolled her eyes. "Love can do that to anyone. Even you."

"Don't I know it," I muttered, moving over to the couch. I tossed her my favorite blanket and grabbed a different one as I got comfy on the other side.

As she settled in, she exclaimed, "Ew! This blanket smells like … tacos? Teriyaki? And something like rotting apple pie?"

I giggled. "I told you, it's been that kind of week."

"It's not cat food, is it? Did you get a cat?" She pretended to look around.

My smile was wistful as I responded, "No, but I have thought about it."

Her eyes were bulging. "Seriously? Here?"

"I don't … you know how I feel about pets. They're cute, but they don't belong at an upper-class resort." I inhaled deeply and blew it out slowly. "Maybe I'll find another place. I don't know."

Her eyebrows were impossibly high on her forehead as she tucked her feet under her. "Wow. I feel like I've missed a ton while I was away."

"A bit," I said, trying to laugh but instead just making a weak crackling sound.

She looked at me seriously. "Mari, are you OK? I saw what happened down there."

I raised my eyebrows. "You mean at the front desk just now?"

"Yeah, I was just in one of the offices nearby, and I heard most of it. Sweetie …"

I stared at the big potted fern across from the couch. "I'd never met her before. Hazel, I didn't even know if she was alive. But also … I kind of stopped caring, long ago." I paused, biting my lip hard. "Does that make me a terrible person?"

"Hell no. I'm no shrink and have zero experience with deadbeat parents, but it sounds like the healthy thing to do." She reached over and patted my shoulder gently. "How are you feeling now?"

I stared at the patterned leaves on the fern, which I'd bought myself as a housewarming present when I moved in here. Finally, I turned to Hazel and said honestly, "It's hard to explain."

Her eyes were wide as she reached for the tissue box. "Aw, Mari, you—you're *crying*. I'm sorry, we don't have to talk about this—"

"It's fine. I'm OK," I assured her.

The odd thing was, I meant it.

The circumstances were far from OK, but *I* was OK. For once, the intensity of feelings didn't cause panic.

She looked at me in astonishment.

"Crying is healthy sometimes, right?" I asked her before sniffling. "And so is talking about feelings—isn't that what you always tell me?"

Her eyes are still huge as she nods slowly. "Of course, a hundred times yes, but I never thought you were listening. You've always insisted showing emotions was a weakness."

I took a deep breath. "Yeah, I have. Because I thought I had to be …" I stopped, wiping another tear from my cheek. "I made these rules for myself. I transformed myself into a person I thought would be accepted. A person who'd never be scorned for being poor or flighty or irresponsible or …"

"Being human?"

My eyes met hers, and I knew I had to give her more. She deserved it. "Yes. You see, my childhood wasn't just difficult. It was … there were times I didn't know if we'd survive. My dad and me. We were poorer than poor. We had nothing—sometimes not even a place to live. My so-called mother abandoned us shortly after I was born, and my father was really sick. Eventually he moved to a nursing home, and I went into foster care. And both before and after that, Hazel, I had nothing. None of the material things but also no *dignity*, no friends. I was ridiculed for being dirt-poor at school, and then the foster families didn't really like me either. And when Dad died, I was devastated. It wasn't until mid-teens that I finally ended up with a decent foster family. They even wanted to adopt me, but I ran away. I know, stupid, right? I should've been honored to call Lisa Jackson my adoptive mother. She ended up being the reason I could afford to buy this place. When she died, she left me a big chunk of her money. I didn't deserve it, but I vowed to put it to good use, to become someone she'd be proud of. Someone Dad would be proud of."

Hazel's eyes were soft. "Oh, Mari, I'm sure he would be proud of you even without the money, but I think I get it."

I nodded, trying to swallow. "And then, Christmas, well, it was Dad's favorite time of year. We always celebrated, even if there was no money. Somehow, I don't know how."

She nodded and squeezed my shoulder. "Oh, I understand now. You couldn't bring yourself to celebrate after that, until this year?"

I started to nod and then shook my head. "Actually, no. I did celebrate Christmas with my foster families after Dad passed, but it wasn't the same. The real reason I boycotted the holiday for the last decade was … Terry."

She raised her eyebrows. "Do tell."

"When he left the resort at the end of his summer vacation, we knew we wouldn't likely have time to meet up during the fall. But we promised each other we'd meet here on Christmas Eve, since we'd both have time off from college." I inhaled deeply and then slowly let the breath out. "I came, and he didn't. Alone and heartbroken on Christmas Eve."

Hazel winced. "Oh no. But since you explained everything about being sabotaged by that bitch—I mean his sister—and then his parents dying, it kind of makes sense why he didn't show."

I nodded. "I don't blame him anymore." I grabbed a tissue and blew my nose. "Anyway, with all the stuff in my childhood plus the mortifying situation with Terry, I just decided I was done being Mariana LaBelle. I desperately wanted to remake myself. When I met you a couple years later, in grad school, I was trying to change, but it was hard. I was still broke, you know? I mean, I had loans to pay for school and was a TA in the business school, but still basically broke. It wasn't until Lisa died—she was my last foster mom—and I got the windfall that I finally had the means to truly remake myself. I'd just gotten my MBA, and you know the rest. I bought the resort, the rest is history. And all the while, I was perfecting what I thought was the perfect or best version of myself I could be …" I trailed off, unsure where to go from here.

"You said 'what you thought was'—past tense?" Her eyes were bright with something I couldn't identify.

"I … maybe I was wrong," I said, looking back at the fern. "All that effort, and I still ended up falling in love with someone who I couldn't be with. And being an emotional mess. Exactly what I'd wanted to avoid." I paused, breathing a little faster before I looked at her. "And do you want to know what's worst of all?"

Hazel gave me a small nod, her eyes glued to mine.

"All that effort, and I ended up just like *her*," I choked out. "I only just met my mother, but anyone can see right away she's a wretched person. The way she looked at me and talked to me … so cool and collected. Also condescending. And *pretentious*. I don't want anything to do with her, and I sure as hell don't want to see her when I look in the mirror every day."

"Mari, Mari, you're nothing like her. You have a kind heart, and you *feel* things and love people and care about things other than money and status. She is none of those things."

"Maybe you didn't see her up close," I said quietly, "but I look just like her. She's just like a slightly older version of me, and she doesn't dye her hair like I do."

Hazel asked hesitantly, "Do you think all along, maybe you were trying to change yourself to win her approval, in case you ever met?"

"No!" I scrunched my face, horrified at the idea. Then I paused to think. Oh, crap. "Maybe. I don't know."

"If not her, then people like her. Pretentious, judgmental, petty people who have nothing better to do than look down on others who are less fortunate, who are only doing their best …" Her voice was barely above a whisper as she said, "People like young Mari."

I swallowed with some difficulty and felt a tear making its way down my cheek, then another. "Yeah, I was. But I think …" I paused, a crease forming between my eyebrows. "I'm *done*, Hazel."

She raised an eyebrow. "Done?"

"Done trying to impress others with some perfect, emotionless version of myself that never really existed anyway. I can't do it anymore. I don't even want to." I shook my head and then steeled my spine as I sat up straight. "And it'll be a cold day in hell before I become like my mother."

My best friend's smile was brighter than I'd seen in a long while, and she nearly knocked me back with the force of her hug.

"I'm so glad, Mari. I never liked seeing you battle with yourself. And you know how many times I've said—"

"You want the real me, I know." The corner of my mouth curved upward on one side. "Well, be careful what you wish for."

She giggled and then abruptly sobered. "What about the resort though? I mean, I know you always felt like you had to maintain a facade for the guests. I suppose anyone in hospitality does …"

I nodded slowly. "True. But … well, maybe I'll start delegating more. I don't have to be so involved in the day-to-day of the business."

"Who even are you?" she exclaimed before hugging me again quickly. "I love that idea." After a moment though, her face fell a bit, and I couldn't read her expression. "Um, I hate to bring this up—"

"Say it."

"Well, what about the Christmas village?"

"What about it?" My brow furrowed in confusion. "I still want it. It's part of my long-term business plan, not just some whimsy."

"But Terry wants it." She pinned me with a serious look. "Most importantly, you want Terry."

I opened my mouth to reply, but I couldn't find any words.

"Don't say you're working on another plan to convince

Jane." She shook her head slightly. "Terry is family, and she's going to give it to him if he wants it. And it seems like he does."

I inhaled sharply. If Jane wanted it to stay in the family, that was likely to happen. But there were still numerous tactics I could try in order to convince her—legal or financial routes that we hadn't gone yet because, well, I wanted this to be organic. Friendly. I had not only money but powerful contacts and advisors on my side.

But none of it mattered.

Terry wanted the village.

He'd lost everything and had to reinvent himself and his future. Owning the village was his future—he was already such an integral part of the community, working at the shop and running the tree farm. And who knew what else?

"If Terry wants the village, I'm not going to stand in his way."

Hazel stared at me for a long time and then finally nodded, a smile overtaking her face.

"You're so happy about this ... after all our hard work?" I was mostly teasing but just a teeny bit annoyed.

"I'm happy because you get to be with Terry!"

I winced. "Haz, I'm really sorry things couldn't work out for you and the cruise guy, but Terry and I aren't—"

"Oh, don't worry about that." She laughed. *Laughed.* "Yeah, I might've gone a bit overboard with thinking he was my soulmate. Sorry about the crazy-making on the phone on Christmas. Really ... I am frustrated with relationships, but a couple days on a French holiday cruise does not a relationship make. No, what I mean is, you and Terry can be together now. Because you're conceding the village."

With my brows furrowed, I started to say, "Wait, I don't think—" I stopped.

Was she right?

"That *was* the reason you told him you couldn't be together, right?"

I nodded. "It was. But I—it wasn't the whole truth. Some of

it was … insecurity."

She scoffed. "Meh, you're always going to have that. We all do." She smiled. "I don't mean to make light of it, sorry. Have you thought about therapy?"

"I always convinced myself I didn't need it, which I can see now is ridiculous." I breathed deeply. "OK, I'll look into it. Mariana 3.0 isn't afraid of talking about her feelings … with a total stranger, right?" I smiled wryly.

"Atta girl." Hazel smiled.

We were silent for a while, and I tried to pin down what, if anything, was still holding me back with Terry.

She waved her hand in front of me. "Get out of your head, Mari. We have some strategizing to do. And I need to get your Christmas presents out of my car!"

My face twisted into cringe. "Oh no, Hazel. I just realized I forgot to wrap a couple of yours that came late. I can—" I stopped when she waved her hand dismissively. Yeah, OK. she didn't care if things were wrapped. But I did. I loved Christmas wrapping.

But then I raised my eyebrows as I remembered the first part of what she said. "We do?"

She rolled her eyebrows. "Of course we do. You're going to win Terry back. From what I've seen though, he's prone to being grumpy. And stubborn. So we'll have to work with that."

"Yes!" My lips curved into a small smile. "Hazel, you always know exactly what I need. So, tell me what to do, wise friend."

Chapter 20

"I told you yesterday, Haz. He wants nothing to do with me," I said glumly, spinning around in my ergonomic office chair to observe the nearly empty space around me. "He hasn't returned my calls or texts. Or emails. Or Instagram messages. Deja vu."

"Hmm, well, I hope you're not thinking of giving up, Mari. I'm sure he just needs some time." I could hear the false optimism in her voice though. In a slightly more natural tone, she asked, "So are you going to hire movers or—"

"Way ahead of you. They're almost done. I have about an hour left before they pack up my office furniture and compter, where I'm still working." I almost wished I was doing the packing myself. At least it would be a good distraction. I needed to stop thinking.

She laughed. "If you must work, why don't you just go to your official office downstairs?"

I sighed. "I don't know. I guess it's just ... letting go is hard." I'd always heard people say that actually, but I'd never really experienced it. In the past, letting go wasn't a difficulty; letting go meant walking away from struggle and bad memories. I was grateful to be able to let go of those parts of my past. But this part ... this was perhaps the first time in my life I'd been proud of something. Granted, it wasn't really a home. Living in a private suite in the resort wasn't the same as having a place to truly call my own, and only mine. I was excited to be finally moving out—especially having found a gorgeous Victorian rental in town that was already vacant—but it was bittersweet all the same.

"Careful, Mari. You're getting sentimental on me," she said in a teasing tone.

I huffed in mock outrage. "No, never!" I sighed again and paused. "I don't want to give up on Terry, but … he's answered one message. One out of … dozens? I don't know. And do you know what he said? 'I can't do this with you.' I mean, he's being pretty clear. It was a waste of time for us to plan all the stuff for me to say to him when he doesn't want to hear any of it."

She was silent for just a moment. "No … he's not *ready* to hear it."

"Well, if that's the case," I said doubtfully, "I can't fix that."

"Oh, but you can!"

"How?"

"Come on, Mari. Haven't you ever heard of a grand gesture? You know, like Kate Beckinsale running across New York to stop John Cusack's wedding, or even Kate Hudson—"

I snickered. "That's for the movies. And for … romantic people. Not me, not real life."

She went quiet for a long moment. "What other option do you have, Mari?" When I was silent, she added, "Maybe more importantly—what do you have to lose?"

A single tear rolled down my cheek as I answered her. "Terry."

Chapter 21

I examined the oak mantle over the hearth. The taller nutcrackers should probably stand together, with the shorter ones on the other side.

After I moved them around, I wrinkled my nose in distaste. No, definitely not. Now it's all asymmetrical. Better to put the tall ones on the inside, short ones on the outside.

I stood back, examining this new configuration. It was improved, yet—

Ring, ring.

My heart lodged in my throat, and my hand flew to my chest. My legs refused to move for a long moment as I tried to catch my breath.

I'd prepared as best I could. I'd just moved in a few days ago, but the house looked great. Well, at least the main floor did. The upstairs was a disaster, but I wouldn't be entertaining anyone upstairs.

Ring, ring.

Crap, I need to go answer that. I lunged forward, nearly tripping over the thick rug in front of the fire.

OK, it's just not going to be possible for me to be low-key and relaxed when I answer the door. I'm going to be panting and sweaty and frazzled.

I tried practicing the positive self-talk I'd been reading about lately. *It's OK, Mariana. Just be yourself. That's all he wants.*

Finally, I took a deep breath and opened the door. He'd been looking to the side, but upon hearing the door, he swung his head in my direction.

Even through the whipping wind outside, I heard his sharp intake of breath. "You."

I tried to smile as brightly as I could. "Me."

Then I watched him turn around and start to walk down the stairs of my front porch. "Wait, don't go! Please."

He ignored me though, and I stood there trying to decide what to do. Grab my boots and follow him? Beg? But as I deliberated, I noticed he wasn't going to the driver's side door. He was heading around the back, opening the door, and … getting the tree out!

He's not leaving! He's just … not too talkative. A little grumpy. OK, I can work with that.

As he approached, I smiled again, though his eyes were on the ground in front of him. "Thank you so much. Could you—"

He leaned the tree against the corner of the porch and then turned as though to leave.

"Wait," I pleaded, putting a hand on his arm as he passed on his way to the stairs. "Terry, please."

He stopped and turned but didn't make eye contact. "You ordered a tree, ma'am. And I've delivered it. Goodbye."

"No, please," I squeezed his arm, feeling the heat as the rest of me shivered on the cold open porch. "Terry, I … I need to talk to you. Please, just give me a few m-minutes."

His jaw tensed, and he stood still for a long moment. "Fine. Speak. You have two minutes."

I swallowed, trying to overcome my fear that anything I say might be the wrong thing, and then he'd leave, forever. "Can we please g-g-go inside?" I asked him, trembling from the freezing wind.

His eyes finally found mine then, and whatever he saw there caused him to groan. His lips were set in a firm line as he replied. "Fine. Two minutes."

I was scared to ask him to carry the tree inside, so I decided I'd try it myself, but before I could take two steps in that direction, he put his thick arm out to block me. "Go inside."

I nodded and turned to go inside, stopping to prop the door open for him. I stood just outside the entryway as he hauled the tree inside.

"Where to?" he asked gruffly when he entered the spacious entryway.

"Follow me," I said, pivoting to walk down the short hallway leading to the living room. But I didn't hear his heavy steps behind me, so I turned back to look. He was removing his boots. I bit my lip to hide a smile. Considerate even when he's angry. But my sense of hope was brief when I noticed he kept his coat and hat on as he picked up the tree to follow me. He wasn't planning to stay long.

Well, he did say two minutes.

So much was riding on those two minutes. My heart felt like galloping horses in my chest as I rounded the curve into the living room, stopping near a pair of chairs and a small table. "Will you sit with me?" I asked, my voice quivering.

He halted when he stepped into the room. I watched his stern expression transform as his eyes swept the large room, which Hazel and I had fully decorated for Christmas. Except one thing.

He pressed his lips together and tightened his jaw. But his eyes betrayed him as he gazed at me in silent wonder.

"All it needs is a Christmas tree, right?"

His eyes shuttered as he nodded and started toward the tree stand.

"You don't have to—" I stopped when I realized he was just going to ignore me. Biting my lip, I hoped the time he spent putting the tree up wouldn't count in my two minutes.

Hopefully he won't hold you to any time limit anyway.

I needn't have worried though, as he worked fast.

"Now I just need to decorate it," I said lightly.

He turned from where he was standing to assess the placement. "OK, two minutes start now."

I attempted to swallow my nerves and pointed to the chair a foot away from mine. "Will you sit?"

He released a long sigh. "Hot in here," he muttered, looking at the fire as he removed his coat and hung it on the chair before sitting down.

This was it. I had spent over a week thinking about what I'd say in this moment.

But it all escaped me. I gazed into his eyes, trying to communicate my feelings, but his were guarded.

"Terry, I made a mistake," I managed to say, my voice betraying my fear that he'd walk away at any moment.

His expression was still blank, but he shifted slightly in his chair.

"I'm sorry ... I know it seems that I-I chose business over you." I waited for him to reply, but he didn't.

I licked my dry lips and took a fortifying breath. "I think I was just overwhelmed. You know what? I don't care anymore. It's yours, Terry. The village, I mean."

The corners of his mouth curled downward as he stared at me and then repeated flatly, "You don't care anymore ... how inspiring." He looked down at his watch. "Not much time left. Anything else?"

"That's not—I didn't mean it like that. The village, it's not for me. It never was, I know that now. But even if it weren't in your family, it wouldn't really matter. My point is really ... I'm making a mess of this. I ..." I stopped, taking a shaky breath.

I looked up from my lap and back up to his face. My eyes might've deceived me, but I could swear a flash of longing passed over his face. He inhaled and exhaled slowly, and for a moment I thought he was going to reach out to me. But, instead, he checked his watch.

For whatever reason, this is when I snapped. "Can you stop *timing* me for just a moment? I'm trying to pour my heart out to you, you stubborn man." And as soon as the words were out, we looked at each other with wide eyes. "Terry, I ... sorry, I have literally never done this before."

Something sparked in his eyes, and we held eye contact. "Ever?" he asked.

"No one else ever made me want to … it's only ever been you, Terry. I think—no, I *know* now that I've always been in love with you. I tried to discard my feelings all those years ago, but I merely buried them. They're lodged so deep—I fear I'll never be free." I took a deep breath. "But now, I don't want to be free of you."

"Mariana," he said, his voice sounding choked. He shook his head, and fear ripped through me.

What if he still walked away?

I couldn't lose him.

Not again.

"There's more," I said quietly, pleading with my eyes for him to listen, to give me a bit more time. "It wasn't the business, really. It was me. I was … I've been struggling with my identity and everything I associate with it."

"I noticed." He shifted in his chair again, this time turning his body more to face me. "What's that really about?"

I opened my mouth and then closed it.

It's OK, you're safe. You can trust him. Show him the real you.

"I think I told you a little before that I didn't have the easiest childhood and grew up in foster care. But what I didn't tell you is … I grew up dirt poor. I mean that literally. Sometimes we slept on the ground. My mother was well off, but she abandoned us after I was born. And my father—he wasn't well enough to take care of me, he couldn't afford to. I *loved* him. He did his very best." I stopped for a brief second, wiping a tear that had found its way down my cheek. "I miss him so much, especially at Christmas."

"I'm sorry, Mariana," he said softly. "I know how hard it is to lose your parents. I didn't know it back then, but I do now."

I tried to swallow, and it was nearly impossible. "I—yeah. He was my everything. When I had nothing." I wiped another tear falling. "I was ridiculed constantly at school because, well, it was obvious we had nothing. It wasn't much better in my first few foster homes. My clothes weren't clean or didn't fit, I couldn't get a decent haircut, and so on … you can imagine. Or maybe you can't, since you grew up in a very different world." At his raised eyebrows, I continued, "No, I don't resent you for that. I never did. You were different from the others I'd known. You saw me as a person, not just a poor girl, a foster child, basically an orphan. You didn't seem to care about my past, my low-class status in the world."

"Oh, I did care," he said, his voice barely above a whisper. "In the sense that I wanted to know all those sides of you. But a few weeks that summer wasn't enough time, not nearly enough."

I exhaled, feeling more tears welling up. "Yes, well—I was ashamed. Your family had looked at me with scorn, and then I thought you wanted nothing to do with me when you went home. I'd had a lifetime of feeling like I wasn't good enough, of feeling shame at who I was. So I decided to change. And that's why I changed my name and the course of my life. I wanted nothing to do with the old Mari, and I closed myself off to all the things I associated with her. Not just being poor and picked on, but everything—being a human with feelings, spontaneity, joy, love, everything. I tried to be the exact opposite of what I'd been. And I succeeded, somewhat. I shut myself off from feeling, as much as humanly possible, and I transformed myself into what I thought was a successful, sophisticated businesswoman."

I looked down at my lap and then back to his eyes, intent on mine. "But then you came back into my life. And I … I found myself reverting back to the old Mariana."

"It scared the hell out of you."

"Yes. *Yes.*"

He looked like he was about to speak, so I waited. "What's changed?"

"Well, other than *you* turning everything on its head? Making me feel all the things I'd tried too hard to squash?" I smiled and then sobered. "Other than that, I met my mother recently. For the first time ever. And if I have anything to say about it, the *only* time ever."

His eyebrows rose. "Wow. What happened?"

"She looks just like me. And she's a condescending snob of the highest order. It took just a minute or so in her presence to realize I was in danger of becoming just like her." I shivered at the thought.

"She sounds awful."

"She was. But I'm so glad we met because I realized … I don't want to be anything like her. I can't. Hazel might've helped a little with that." I offered a weak smile.

He nodded, a patient, open expression having replaced the hardened one from earlier.

"I'm telling you this because—well, I do want you to know me better, but also because it's a big part of why I believed I couldn't be with you." I breathed in, my heart racing. "You fell for the old Mari, and I have spent so many years denying her existence. You made me question everything."

He stood then and walked over to me, taking my hands to bring me to my feet. "I absolutely did fall for the Mari of ten years ago, but guess what?"

"What?" I managed to say, disoriented by his proximity.

He tipped my chin up to gaze at him. "This winter, I fell for you all over again. Whatever version of you this is, I don't care. I just want you. It's all I've ever wanted," he said, his voice breaking at the end of that sentence.

"Oh, Terry," I said, flinging my arms around him before stepping back suddenly. "Can you forgive me?"

"Nothing to forgive," he mumbled, placing both of his hands on my cheeks with a feather-light touch.

I felt my lips start to form a smile. "I guess I'll forgive *you* for being so stubborn."

He grinned. "I'm gonna need that forgiveness every day, I think."

A sarcastic response was on the tip of my tongue, but it was smothered by his mouth.

Not a light kiss, but a soul-searing one, communicating ten long years worth of missed opportunities. My lips parted as he kissed me deeply and tangled his hands in my hair. My own hands tugged off his hat and then clutched the back of his neck, pulling him closer.

I broke away with a gasp. "I could do this all day, I think."

He started nibbling on my neck then, finding my racing pulse. "I think I could do it forever."

I smiled briefly before his lips found mine again. His hands found my waist, but before he could pull me closer, I placed my hand on his pounding heart and pulled my head back, just a few inches. "I can't really take you upstairs …"

His brow wrinkled in question, and then he laughed huskily. "It's OK. I can wait."

"No, I mean, every room upstairs is just a pile of boxes. I just moved in two days ago, and I've spent all my time working on the main floor."

"All for me?"

I raised an eyebrow. "You think I'd do all this for you?"

"Mmmm," he said, kissing my jaw, and I forgot what we were talking about for a moment. Was this really happening? "Well, that looks like a cozy thick rug by the fire. What do you say we make this a memorable Christmas Eve?"

"Even though it's not—"

He put his finger to my lips as he led me over to the stately old fireplace. "Shh, Mariana. It'll be our tradition. Christmas in January."

Epilogue

Six months later

My mouth curved into a satisfied smile as my eyes scanned the scene around me. The attention of the crowd was all focused on the man next to me on the small stage decorated in red, green, and silver garland and tinsel, and I squeezed his strong hand.

"Welcome, everyone, to the inaugural Christmas in July fest. I'm Terry Grant." One irresistable smile had the crowd cheering. "And if you don't already know this amazing woman, this is the lady of the castle, Mariana LaBelle Northam."

I chuckled softly to myself, remembering how I used to hate the castle thing. But it grew on me, along with everything else about Shipsvold. The town seemed to be embracing me, even though I'm not sure I deserved it. But in the past six months, I'd tried to make up for my neglect. Having Terry by my side made it easy, but I was determined to win people over on my own merits. By being myself, through and through. Not some idealized, unapproachable version. Somehow, it seemed to be working.

Terry had continued speaking, but he looked over just then and caught me staring. I smiled.

I had nothing to hide.

I adored him, and he knew it. Everyone else soon would too. We were planning to announce our new business merger, combining the resort with the Christmas village and tree farm. We were calling it Grantham Hospitality and Event Services.

But that could wait.

I cleared my throat and tugged on his red and green shirt. "Terry." I reached into the pocket of my skirt with a secret smile and then started to clasp his hands, which were damp. Or maybe mine were? It was, after all, 85 degrees outside.

With his hands in mine, I started to lower my body to kneel on the tinsel-covered floor of the stage. But before my knee touched the floor, his eyes flashed, and he tugged me upward. "Oh my! Mariana, you can't. No, you're not—"

"Oh, but I am," I said, my smile growing as I tried to kneel again, but he clasped my hands and then my elbows firmly.

"You're going to ruin—"

My face fell, and something inside started to deflate. But he cupped my chin with gentle fingers, forcing me to look up at him.

His eyes were twinkling as he shook his head and grinned. "You're ruining *my* plans to propose."

My eyes went wide as he stuck his hand in his jeans pocket. He—*he* was going to propose to *me*?

I tried to catch my breath as I took in the sight of this man, remembering I'd almost lost him forever.

If not for Christmas, I might have.

I took a deep breath as he was still fiddling around in his pocket. "Terry, will you—"

"Marry me, Mari."

"Terry! This was supposed to be my proposal. I ... you—"

"You're so stubborn. And I love it, and everything about you." His eyes were shining, and I couldn't find the words to interrupt him. "Just say you'll marry me."

My lips twisted at the corners as I pretended to think about it. "On one condition."

His eyebrows lifted, and it was then I noticed the silence surrounding us. Mouths were gaping, even from Nina and Hazel on a bench near the front. The crowd was hanging on our every word. I flashed a sheepish smile at Jane, who nodded to me with a slight smile. Turning back to Terry, I stared into his deep, dark eyes, which felt like home. This man and this place I loved—it was home. Finally, I was home.

"I'll marry you on Christmas Eve."

Acknowledgments

They say it takes a village to raise a child—or in fiction, it takes a whole team to put your book baby in the hands of readers. But for me, what it really took was a partner who stood beside me every step of the way. Mr. Highbury, you've supported me throughout my journey to publishing my first book, just as you've been by my side for everything else that matters.

I'm so grateful to my cover designer, Stefanie Fontecha of Beetiful Book Covers; my proofreader, Jessica Hay; my web designer, Emily Rusu of The Writer's Site; my marketing/PR consultant, Amanda Kerr; and my wonderful ARC readers and street team. I also want to thank Ingrid Pierce, a published romance author and previously my mentor from the Contemporary Romance Writers organization. Her mentoring and editorial feedback on a different manuscript were invaluable in helping me to improve my craft (and she's a certified coach now, so you can look her up and learn from her too).

I wouldn't be writing without my online writer and reader groups. The Moms Who Write group got me writing again a couple years back after I'd nearly abandoned an Austen-inspired series that I'd started a decade ago. Countless other groups for romance readers and writers have given me encouragement, inspiration, ideas, laughs, and friendships in recent years. Readers, you are my favorite kind of people. Thank you for giving this new author a chance!

And to circle back to family ... Mom and Grandma, thanks for reading a draft of my first book and being gentle in your feedback. And although I can't thank my children or my cats or my bird for giving me time to write or other resources, they give me something far more important every day: inspiration. And, of course, love.

I believe in second chances. And sometimes third or fourth. As many as it takes because when you find the one, it is worth every challenge that came before and every difficulty you haven't yet faced. Mr. Highbury, my deepest gratitude for your unwavering love and support, without which this book wouldn't be published (or written). Thank you!

A Humble Request

Thank you for taking the time to read and review! Even brief reviews mean so much to independent authors.

If you loved this book, please consider leaving a review or rating:

- *Amazon*
- *Goodreads*
- *BookBub*

If you didn't like the book but want to offer feedback, feel free to email me at **alana@alanahighbury.com**. I'd like to hear more about what didn't work for you. Whether it's something I can fix or just not a fit, I'd be glad to hear from you!

Readers, you are my favorite kind of people. Thank you.

About the Author

Alana Highbury is the author of *Meet Me on Christmas Eve*, Snowed In on Valentine's Day, and the forthcoming *Dance with Me on New Year's Eve*. She also has a trio of Jane Austen-inspired novels releasing in 2025. Her novels blend rom-com, contemporary romance, and women's fiction. When she's not writing, you can find her reading, playing board games, cross stitching, or hanging out with her family, which includes a writerly husband and children, two beautiful, lazy cats, and a feisty cockatiel.

With master's and bachelor's degrees in English, Alana has worked in professional writing and editing roles for two decades, but she's been an avid fan of romance fiction even longer.

Check out her website at https://alanahighbury.com, or follow her on social media:
https://www.facebook.com/alanahighbury.author
https://www.instagram.com/alanahighbury_author/
https://www.goodreads.com/alanahighbury
https://amazon.com/author/alanahighbury
https://www.bookbub.com/authors/alana-highbury

Books In This Series

Love & Holidays

Meet Me On Christmas Eve

A second-chance romance set at Christmas in a snowy small town

Snowed In On Valentine's Day

An enemies-to-lovers romance with two neighbors stranded together in a snowstorm

Dance With Me On New Year's Eve

An enemies-to-lovers, secret-identity romance where our shy protagonist finds love and a fresh start

Printed in Great Britain
by Amazon